AMUSING TALE OF

Battlefields House

Diane x
Davies.

THE AMUSING TALE OF
Battlefields House

DIANE DAVIES

BROWN DOG BOOKS

First published 2025

Published under licence by Brown Dog Books and
The Self-Publishing Partnership Ltd, 10b Greenway Farm,
Bath Rd, Wick, nr. Bath BS30 5RL, UK

www.selfpublishingpartnership.co.uk

ISBN printed book: 978-1-83952-926-9

Cover design by Andrew Prescott
Internal design by Andrew Easton

Printed and bound in the UK

This book is printed on FSC® certified paper

MIX
Paper | Supporting responsible forestry
FSC® C013604
www.fsc.org

DEDICATION

This book is dedicated to Ian whose enthusiasm and encouragement has been instrumental in helping to bring about BATTLEFIELDS HOUSE.

We shared the journey together.

Also my wonderful family Craig and Katie, Mitchell and Clare and inspirational and much loved Grandchildren

Taylor, Jack, and Ellis Davies

PREFACE

Battlefields House is the amusing tale of the McKenzie family, and their sudden decision to move to a shared country residence not far from Bath. But after moving in, the McKenzie's soon realise that the other residents at the Battlefields mansion are made up of an international group of individuals who have their own agendas on how Battlefields should be run.

After Adam is coerced into becoming Chairman of the management committee he has to juggle the finances, garden contracts, roof repairs and cantankerous residents while Nicola is focussed on making friends, decorating their new apartment and helping Adam to keep the peace between recalcitrant individuals who make up the eclectic mix of residents at Battlefields House.

CHAPTER 1

FAIROAKS

The phone rang several times before Adam picked it up; it was Rosie the estate agent. My husband's face lit up with a huge smile, which stretched from ear to ear, which when you have the McKenzie ears is a very wide smile indeed. Our house had been on the market for three months and we had only one viewing so far. The first and only couple to view had made a very good offer, but unfortunately still had a property to sell. Therefore, we had left our lovely property on the market with an understanding that if no new offers were on the table, number 3 Fairoaks would be theirs. Three months later and still no new viewings, we were beginning to think the housing market had ground to a halt, when out of the blue this call from Rosie came through.

'The Harper couple have sold to a cash buyer,' my husband whispered, covering the mouthpiece of the phone, as he punched the air with his left fist.

'Mmmmm,' Adam's voice continued, 'that's great news, but six weeks doesn't give us a lot of time to find our next home,' he said, looking a little perplexed.

After the initial strong fist pump, Adam's hand went to his

thick black hair, and pulled his fringe back, a thing he rarely did, and only ever when he was feeling stressed. His hand then went to his heart, which was obviously beating a little faster than usual, and was not to his liking.

We had foolishly led ourselves into a false state of security, thinking there would be months to start looking for a new humble abode, when the Harpers finally sold. Not so!

The odd glance at the property paper and the occasional flick through Rightmove on the internet had not turned up our ideal residence and over time we had become too complacent, leaving us in the situation we now found ourselves. Possibly homeless!

It transpired that the cash buyer was keen, if not insistent, that they wanted to move quickly. Therefore, if we wanted the sale to go through, we would have to vacate our property within six weeks.

The wheels in my head started turning – could it be possible that we would be leaving our family home in just six weeks? We had lived at Fairoaks for the past twenty years, a large four-bedroomed Wimpey estate house, with a beautiful mature oak tree at the end of the garden.

The tree had been planted long before the house was built, and had been listed as a protected species; I had loved it since we first moved in. It had been home to many nesting birds for over twenty years. I had watched the tight buds in spring open, bursting forth with new life. In summer the large leaves cast a dappled shade that stretched into our garden, creating a cool patch where I could sit and watch our sons playing. And in the autumn, I had seen the leaves turn golden, catching the last rays of the sun before winter crept in. I had spent many an hour raking the gilded crisps from the lawn, bagging them up with the help of my energetic sons. The tree had been a silent witness to our family comings and goings, such happy memories. Beyond the great oak there was a parkland area, with gated playground, a climbing frame, swings and a slide perfect for our two young sons to take their football, meet up with their friends and let off steam.

Fairoaks, as it became fondly known to us, had been the perfect home to our family but now our sons were young adults and one had already left home, so it was time to move on. Finding a new place for just the two of us and our youngest son of nineteen was going to be the next challenge. We would take all those wonderful memories, keeping them close to our hearts, and turn the page ready for a new exciting chapter in our lives.

There would be neighbours to say goodbye to, friends to hug and promises made to keep in touch, newspapers to cancel, grass to mow and the loft to clear. Twenty years of loft accumulation – the thought was terrifying! – and we had not found a property that we wanted to call our new home.

The move was pencilled in the diary for the fourteenth of February so any romantic notions of breakfast in bed, chocolates and champagne, or a valentine's night away in a luxury hotel went well and truly out the window.

The next five weeks and six days went by in a flash. The loft was systematically cleared of all the bric-a-brac, which either went to family or friends, or to the chosen charities in Keynsham, our local town centre. I became a regular visitor on the High Street, hauling big black sacks up and down the road, trying to offload the huge amount of McKenzie clothing, toys, unused crockery, bed linen and countless football boots in various sizes, trying not to overburden any one charity shop with more black sacks than they could cope with. Spreading the McKenzie baggage evenly between The Heart Foundation, Dorothy House Hospice and Oxfam. I became known as the black bag lady of Keynsham.

I was given the evil eye on many occasions when I popped my head round the shop door and announced 'It's me again!' only to produce from behind my back yet another black sack bursting at the sides. I think the charity shop ladies were glad to see the back of me when I eventually stopped turning up.

As our departure day drew nearer, we contacted a removal company called 'We Like to Move It' who were due to pick up our furniture and belongings at 9 a.m. on the Tuesday morning.

We had rushed around to see our lovely friends and neighbours to say our fond farewells, several who were genuinely sorry to see us go. Some over the years had found my two young sons rather annoying, when footballs had continually landed in their gardens, breaking pots and flattening flowerbeds.

One neighbour in particular, an elderly friend, Phyllis, who lived directly opposite, shed a tear. Having seen our boys Thomas and Ben grow up over the years, she had become fond of us as a family – joining in family celebrations, Christmas-present-giving and popping in for an update on the local gossip, for which she was infamous. From the local library to the doctors' surgery, from the bus stop to the post office, Phyllis was in the know and spread the word near and far. She was a dear friend and I would miss her tall tales and banter.

Kindly she had always come over with a little brown envelope on the boys' birthdays, which they loved as it contained a five-pound note and a funny card, and the boys had always enjoyed taking over a piece of home-made birthday cake to her as a thank you.

I would miss her and that mischievous twinkle in her eye, especially when she had a morsel of local gossip to impart. After giving her an enormous hug, I promised that I would keep in touch. 'After all, we are only moving ten miles away,' I told her.

The search for our next home had begun in earnest after Rosie's phone call a few weeks earlier. We had scanned the internet just in case our dream house had been added to the 'FOR SALE' property list. Numerous estate agents had been contacted, hoping that they might have that gem of a house perfect for us. New property alerts were initiated on the internet. Friends sent emails listing brand-new builds in their local areas that might prove promising, and family members were dragged into helping locate any likely house within a ten-mile radius of our desired location that might fit the bill. Everything was considered: three-storey town houses, cottages, flats overlooking the marina at Portishead – very nice indeed, but not what we were looking for.

We wanted something a little different, a home with character, high ceilings and above all, I wanted a view from the back garden. My husband's list of must-haves was interesting, rural and quiet. No neighbours with barking dogs, and the icing on the cake, he had said on more than one occasion, would be enough lawn to require a sit-on lawn mower.

Two weeks after Rosie's phone conversation, we had seriously considered moving into rented accommodation, as we had not been able to find a suitable property to call home. But one Friday evening after dinner, Adam dropped the local property paper in my lap, sat down next to me, promising to load the dish washer and agreeing to search for our son's golf clubs that resided in our loft space, after a little snooze. He instantly put his head back and promptly fell asleep next to me. I turned the pages of the paper carefully, trying not to awaken my sleeping spouse, but finally gave up, put my head on his comfortable shoulder and fell asleep too.

An hour later, as promised, the dish washer was loaded and spun into action, gurgling and gushing as it cleaned our dinner dishes. Adam unhooked the loft ladder and climbed into the cobwebbed interior of the space above the kitchen ceiling and roof that we called the loft.

After numerous mutterings of 'We must get a light fixed up here,' and 'I can't find them,' and 'Is Tom sure they are up here?' I retreated to the lounge, where I sat down to peruse the rest of the property paper.

Then I spotted it!

A small insignificant advert caught my attention. It read,

Battlefields House
Country House Apartment
No Onward Chain
Two Generous Bedrooms
Rural Location near Lansdown Golf Course
Close to Bath

This is an unusual property and rarely comes on the market.
A beautiful building set down a driveway that is

> **split into apartments, with communal parking and allocated garage. This is a rare find in a unique and beautiful setting that will delight those looking for something quite special but a little out of the ordinary.**

It did not say a sit-on lawn mower is required to keep the grass in check, but it did meet most requirements, as far as I was concerned.

My heart started pumping, my mouth went dry, and the cogs started to whirl in my head. I rushed to the bottom of the ladder, shouting up to Adam, 'I think I've found it!'

'I thought you said they were in the attic!' came a curt reply from the dark abyss above. 'You said the clubs were definitely up here.'

'NO!' I shouted excitedly, 'I think I've found a property.' His head dropped below the hatch door and he eyed me suspiciously.

'Where?' he said.

I explained quickly that here was an apartment in a manor house for sale, situated on the top of Lansdown near the golf course. The mention of the words *golf course* brought my husband down the ladder faster than a fireman down a fireman's pole, almost splitting his chinos at the crotch, accompanied by that grin, spreading from ear to ear again.

'Really,' he said. 'Shall we book to go and see it tomorrow? Let's telephone Rosie and book a viewing in the morning.'

No mention of *How much? How many bedrooms?* or *does it have a garage?*

My dear husband was obviously transfixed with the fact that it was within walking distance of the local golf course!

Well, if that was his only real priority in life I would do exactly what he suggested and immediately phone Rosie at Davis and Way, who were coincidentally acting for the vendor for this property, to make an appointment to view the next day at eleven o'clock. At the back of my mind, I was wondering why Rosie had not brought this property to our attention; after all, it ticked so many of our boxes!

I left him at the bottom of the ladder and rushed off to make the call to Rosie that could change our lives forever. I found her name under R in the telephone book. Adam always laughed at my unusual way of filing names in the little black book, stating that Rosie should be filed under E for estate agent, but as usual, I had my own strange way of doing things that only I understood. R was for Rosie, who I knew to be the only Rosie in the book, and she was the Estate Agent!

I located her mobile number, listening as the phone connected. 'Davis and Way, Rosie speaking,' she said into the device. After explaining who I was, and the fact that we were interested in the property at Lansdown that was on their books, she went quiet, then uttered "That's Battlefields House?' After a long pause she said, 'You want to view Battlefields House?' She sounded a little surprised, then said, in her official estate-agent's voice, 'Of course! I'll make an appointment with the vendor for you tomorrow morning at eleven o'clock. That will be Mr Batley, apartment three, at Battlefields House, Lansdown.' And so, it was arranged!

After returning to the attic a second time and finally locating the much-sought-after golf bag and clubs, my husband descended from the hatch at a more sedate rate, covered in cobwebs, and joined me in the lounge.

After reading the description of the apartment, he agreed it fitted most of our requirements but was understandingly confused that the advert was a little short on detail. There was also no picture of the apartment, no pictures of the interior rooms, and no picture of Battlefields itself. Very puzzling!

The laptop was produced, as Adam being Adam, set out on a mission to discover more detail about this elusive Battlefields property. He bought up the Davis and Way website and searched for the apartment, but could not seem to find out much more than we already knew. There surely must be a photograph or more detail for us to view, but no.

'Rosie said something about it being a listed building,' I volunteered, trying hard to sound upbeat. 'Grade two listed,' I said, 'so perhaps that's why there are no pictures,' I suggested feebly. My husband gave me the look he always does when he knows I'm waffling, and in cricket terms, 'batting on a sticky wicket'. But his curiosity had got the better of him and he wanted to find out more. He was not going to be beaten, he was Adam and he would prevail.

Headings on Google under *Grade II listed buildings, Battlefields House, Lansdown, Bath* produced one black-and-white image taken back in 1972 of a gothic-style country mansion. The image was a little blurry and taken from a long distance. It looked as if the building had a huge conservatory built on the side, or perhaps an orangery, the likes of which I had seen at Dyrham Park recently, housing lemon trees and exotic plants. 'How exciting!' I said 'Our own oranges and lemons, and look at all that lawn – you would have a field day out there with your sit-on mower.'

We did a little more research and found an article which read, *Originally built as Lilliput Castle by John Wood the Elder, Battlefields House was developed around it by Charles Harcourt Masters. The building had been renovated in 1970 by Charlie Bennet, a property developer.*

There was a black-and-white image of Mr Charlie Bennet, smoking a large cigar, with Battlefields behind him in the distance. He looked like an Arthur Daley type character from the 1970s TV programme *Minder*. He was even sporting a pinstripe suit and a felt trilby hat!

The information we found had us hooked. We had to go and see this property, even if it turned out to be on a fool's errand.

After all it wouldn't hurt, would it?

CHAPTER 2

BATTLEFIELDS HOUSE

Morning came, and after a restless night thinking about the property, we enjoyed a sizzling treat of bacon, eggs, one thick pork sausage each and a circle of Adam's favourite black pudding. This was followed by a piece of freshly sliced crusty loaf (toasted to perfection), lashings of Cornish butter and thinly sliced orange marmalade, oh and a strong filtered Taylor's Colombian coffee, before we set off to find the elusive Battlefields House.

The satnav took us up Tog Hill and wound its way up long, leafy country lanes out of the city and on past the well-known golf club, Tracy Park. At the bend in the road, the view opened out and miles of open countryside could be seen in every direction.

We pulled in to admire the view and sat for ten minutes trying hard to locate our little house in the far distance, which we would be sadly leaving behind. Then Adam spotted the green metal sign that Rosie had told us to look out for.

BATTLEFIELDS HOUSE
PRIVATE DRIVE

We have our own private drive, I thought to myself.

After turning into the drive, we followed a winding lane covered by overhanging chestnut trees, and as we wound our way slowly down, we caught glimpses of the grey, gothic building in the distance, which was Battlefields House. Through the trees we could see extensive green lawns surrounding the building, plenty of grass for my dear husband to trim to perfection when he invests in his sit-on lawn mower.

The lawn rose into banks surrounding the property, which were covered with freshly shooting wild garlic leaves, and ancient ferns covered the ground beneath the trees either side of the winding driveway. One high bank was overgrown with stinging nettles.

Probably a nature conserve for butterflies, I thought romantically.

A semicircle of huge oak trees wrapped their way round two thirds of the property, creating an imposing backdrop to the building. One lonely pine tree, that must have been over a hundred years old, was growing very close to the front of the building, looking slightly out of place. It cast its spiky shadow across the battlements. I gave a little shudder, but instantly shook off the feeling of someone walking over my grave.

As we drew closer to the building and out of the shady drive, there in all its faded glory was the house we had come to see! We could not help being impressed by the size of the building – it had been very grand in its time.

A second bank, this time of meadow-like flowers flowed down another embankment towards the front of the house, into what can only be described as a lawned terrace area. Perhaps, once upon a time, it had been an area that housed a tennis court, or a sunken natural pool. It would have been quite something in its heyday. We stood gazing at the sight before us, mesmerised by all that we saw.

There were turrets and battlements at the top of the building, the roof sloped off in several different directions covering various heights and levels. There were stone-built chimney pots individually designed, which towered above the building, old slated roof tiles, which appeared to be original, as were the casement windows that looked out at us like steely glass eyes glinting in the sunlight. At each corner of the battlements there were grotesque gargoyles looking down on us, ugly little men or animals carved from stone, weather-beaten; some had lost parts of their anatomy, causing them to look even more menacing.

We looked at each other and laughed out loud, both wondering what we had let ourselves in for.

After leaving the car in the car park, we walked over to the front of the house. A low stone veranda, beset with hand-carved stone finials covered with lichen, led us up two steps to the magnificent arched, oak front doors. Large black rivets ran down the front of each of the doors and matching black hinges held them in their ancient frames. The weathered oak shone in the sunlight protected from the winter storms by a glossy coat of yacht varnish. There was no letter box or door knocker with which to attract attention, but my husband pointed out a metal keypad screwed on to the doorframe to the right of the entrance. It listed flats 1–8. By each number in handwritten ink were the surnames of each resident.

1. HARDING
2. WHIPSNAKER
3. BATLEY
4. CUMMINGS
5. MATHER
6. JONES
7. ROMANO
8. JONES

Romano sounded a little Italian, Jones sounded English with perhaps Welsh ancestry, Whipsnaker sounded like a middle-aged lady of the night but I wondered silently if number 3 would soon have the McKenzie name written in black ink next to it. I stepped forward and pressed the buzzer for number three, and after what seemed an endless amount of time, the intercom crackled into life and an elderly voice came through.

'Yes,' the voice said, which was only just audible, 'what do you want?' I stepped closer to the intercom and spoke clearly, introducing ourselves, but after what seemed like an eternity, the elderly voice came through again.

'Yes, who is it?', then after another long pause, 'Bloody thing . . . never works!'

'Do you think he can hear us?' I said out loud.

'Not sure' Adam replied, so he pressed the buzzer again.

We received no crackles and no acknowledgement this time, so after several minutes and by now, quite unsure how to proceed, we contemplated pressing a different button, at least to summon any other resident who might let us into the building.

I peered through one of the small square glass panes in the

window next to the door. The hallway was dimly lit and appeared empty, but gradually I could make out a slow-moving, blurred figure, descending into the hall. The ghostly spectre came towards the front door and as I moved away from the window, we heard a large key turn in the lock.

The heavy door slowly opened and a wraithlike figure peered out at us suspiciously. He looked us up and down from behind the doorframe, pressed his spectacles back on to his wizened old face, as if he needed a clearer look, and appeared to contemplate shutting the door again.

We quickly introduced ourselves before he had time to close the door in our faces, and explained that we had come to view the apartment. Suddenly, it was as if a light had been switched on, and he seemed to recall the appointment made the previous day by the estate agent, but he couldn't recall her name.

After opening the heavy oak door just wide enough to let us in, he shuffled his way slowly to the back of the hallway towards a wide staircase that seemed to float on thin air.

This was Walter Batley, proprietor and elderly resident of Battlefields House. He was dressed in dark green baggy corduroy trousers and his long-knitted cream cardigan swamped his thin body and hung down to his knees. It was as if he had shrunk in the wash, but his clothes had not. On his feet were thick woollen socks that were housed in burgundy leather slip-on slippers. Definitely a class above the rest of his attire.

'Cantilever,' Mr Batley muttered over his shoulder, and pointed with an extremely long finger (with an even longer finger nail attached at the end) to the stairway we were about to ascend. 'Don't give a mind to the carpet, it's on the agenda for the next management committee meeting,' he continued. I glanced down to the rust-coloured carpet and hoped it was on the agenda to be replaced sooner rather than later! Treading carefully up the stairs behind Walter Batley, I noticed the stair covering was faded and worn, not bad enough to call dangerous, but not far off. The sunlight filtering down on to the cantilevered stairway came from an arched dome of glass high up above the plaster ceiling; it appeared to be an original skylight. The blue sky could be seen outside and a few fluffy white clouds floated by. Ever optimistic, I took this to be a good omen.

As we rose higher Mr Batley pulled himself up most of the way by holding on to the black wrought-iron railings that ran the entire length of the spiralling stairway, gradually reaching the door to his apartment. It was obviously quite a struggle for him to mount the stairs, and I could understand why he wanted to move.

Walter took out a brass Chubb key from his pocket, unwinding it from his crumpled handkerchief, and turned the key in the lock.

'Can't be too careful – thieving bastards here, you know!' he said.

Adam looked at me and raised his left eyebrow, and we both stifled a laugh. We were finding the whole experience rather comical, when suddenly, as the door opened and Walter gave it a hearty push, he let out what can only be described as a little 'tree-frog fart'. My lungs nearly burst as I tried to contain an explosive laugh. My husband's hand shot across my mouth, hoping to stop what could have turned into an embarrassing moment. We didn't want to offend the old man.

My ribcage was heaving up and down as I tried to control my laughter. I forced the air back down into my lungs and retreated down to the hallway to try and compose myself, leaving Adam to make some excuse as to my whereabouts.

Literally running through the hallway, leaving the front door ajar, I sought refuge in the car until I could redeem some self-control. After my laughter had finally subsided, I sat there wondering whether to return to the apartment, when I caught sight of Adam in the upstairs apartment window, beckoning me to join him. He had saved the day, apparently, explaining that I had received an urgent phone message, and thought it better to take the call in the privacy of the car, down in the car park. Very plausible, I thought!

After returning upstairs, I joined Walter and Adam in the lounge, which proved to be a high-ceiling, hexagonally shaped room. There was a fairy-tale turret accessed by three little stone steps in the corner of the room, which looked out over the lawned area of the garden. The car park could also be seen, where our silver automobile sat, waiting patiently for us like a trained puppy dog waiting for its master.

It was a charming addition to the room, with small casement windows on three sides and an old wooden rocking chair with a cushion that had lost its plumpness and pretty red tassels many years ago, the chair faced the lovely view from behind the glass frame. It was quite unique!

Before I could say anything, Walter shuffled across to the other side of the room and stood by the sizeable windows, which stretched almost two thirds of the way along the opposite wall. 'JUST LOOK AT THAT VIEW!' he almost shouted as he gestured with his left arm towards the landscape out of the window. 'Quite magnificent, don't you think?'

Could this be our new home or was I getting carried away with delusions of grandeur? Could we live here? It would certainly be very different from number 3 Fairoaks. It would be an exciting place to reside; living here could be an amazing experience. I was warming to the idea! But was my husband? He had not uttered a word since we had come into the room.

Walter Batley was obviously trying to emphasise that with the apartment came this fantastic outlook. We had to agree with him, it was indeed magnificent. I thought the view alone was worth every penny Walter was asking for his home, but I had to stop letting my heart rule my head – something my husband was always telling me – and think carefully if we wanted this to be our new home.

On the walls of the great room hung ancient, sepia-tinted boundary maps encased in gilt frames. A pair of old wooden muskets sat crossing each other, pointing up towards the ceiling, above what was once a fine marble fireplace. This was now boarded up and a large glass vase of dried and silk flowers resided in the place of an absent roaring log fire. I supposed the transportation of firewood would have proved just too much for Walter these days, but I could imagine what it would be like sitting in front of a hot crackling fire, toasting your toes, while the wind and rain beat down outside.

'Perhaps you would like some tea?' said Walter, bringing me back suddenly to the present, 'and some cake.' We accepted his offer warmly and sat down on the leather burgundy Chesterfield settee. Walter left us and wandered off to the kitchen, and while he was absent, Adam got up and moseyed over to the sizeable bookcase that leant against the back wall.

'Take a look at these titles,' he gasped, pulling out a plain black book. '*Before they are Hanged*, by Joe Abercrombie! And how about this,' as he pointed to another title. '*Death Keeps Me Awake* by Wolfgang Zumdick . . . and this! *Postcolonial Melancholia* by Paul Gilroy. Walter certainly likes his light reading material – that's enough to keep even me awake at night!'

I immediately saw the funny side and pointed to an oil painting hanging on the wall in one of the alcoves. 'What about that then?' I whispered. There halfway up and not quite squarely hung, was a portrait of a young boy in a red button-down tunic. I rose from the Chesterfield and stepped closer to get a better look. The painting was in oil, dark and strange; it appeared not to have been completed, as several sections of the overall image were missing. The boy was dressed in blue velvet with lace trims to his collar and cuffs and seemed to seep into the oily background like a ghost disappearing into thin air. Sitting next to the blond-haired child by his feet, which were also incomplete was a King Charles spaniel gazing longingly up at the boy, patiently waiting for his attention. The painting was not held in a frame as you would expect, but had been painted on a thick board, with the edges of the wood coloured in black. It was all very eerie! I would be glad to see that removed from the wall and packed away in Mr Batley's removal van when he left the premises.

While we waited for Walter to return with a much-needed cup of tea, we sat for a few moments in silence, each taking in the surroundings of this elderly, eccentric old gentleman's collection of unusual, eclectic antiques and all the found treasures he had accumulated over his time here at Battlefields.

The tiled floor was covered by a huge faded Persian rug, its fringed edge missing in several places; it was threadbare in patches, having been trodden on and worn through over many years.

The plaster ceiling, which was exceptionally high and in great proportion to the rest of the room, was centred by a huge brass candelabrum that dropped into the room like a graceful ballerina in a tutu, but the brass was now tarnished after years of neglect.

The drapes that framed the tall windows were full-length red damask and of a quality that would have been expensive back in the day when they had first adorned the windows. But after decades of unfiltered sun exposure, they had sadly faded to match the once beautiful Persian rug on the floor.

My view from the settee, out through the glass window, was one of the tops of the trees that surrounded Battlefields House. They were of an age that matched the two-hundred-year-old property and some were even older, having been part of an ancient wood once upon a time. Decades had gone by and the trees had grown up, hiding what must have been spectacular views from the apartment window, breathtaking views over the countryside, and beyond.

There were three large grey cumbersome radiators on three walls of the room – the type I had seen in our local church – but I consoled myself that at least the apartment had a heating system! Things were looking rosy!

Eventually Mr Walter Batley Esquire could be heard padding slowly back down the hallway, bringing a tray of tinkling china and walnut cake for our consumption.

He came through the heavily glossed white, overly large

door, into the room and placed the tray a little shakily in front of us, on the long low wooden coffee table, at which we both sat.

'Help yourselves to tea,' he said. 'I'm a little shaky these days when it comes to tea-pouring.'

Two little pink wafer biscuits, the sort we had as children on special occasions like birthdays, were sitting next to two thinly sliced pieces of walnut cake. The thin bone china cups and saucers with gilt rims were placed next to each other on the tray, with a sweet little sugar bowl and matching jug.

As we sat sipping our kettle-hot tea, Walter had a character change right in front of us – he became a salesman!

'I expect you have been admiring my collection of Delftware,' he said, moving to the alcove behind the door to the hallway. There were at least twenty large blue-and-white serving dishes festooning the wall, each one twice the size of a dinner plate. They were hung by brass wires that clamped the sides of each piece of crockery like a British bulldog clinging on to a meaty bone. A few plate-edges had succumbed to the pressure caused by the extended length of time they had been hanging there, and a few hairline cracks had started to appear.

'Each one of these a little treasure. My late wife, Alamina, was the collector really; we travelled the world in our lifetime together, dealing in antiques, and she always had a good eye for a bargain,' he said. 'We picked these up in Holland at an antiques fair, many moons ago, but I'm willing to let you have them . . . at the right price!' As he said this, he winked at me with his slightly faded-blue left eye. I could imagine that once upon a time our Walter had been quite a lady's man with a twinkle in his then bright blue left eye.

He continued, 'They are an investment, you see, always increasing in value. You can't go wrong buying them from me.'

Adam perked up and asked how much Walter was asking for them.

'Two hundred pounds each, but those on the bottom are very rare and I'd be asking five hundred each for those,' he said, growing more excited as he tried to entice Adam into purchasing a job lot.

Adam enquired if Walter would be open to offers, but Walter was disinclined to bargain for his crockery, so we let it drop and moved on to the kitchen area, where we were in for yet another surprise, or a shock.

The first thing I noticed was the kitchen floor. It was covered in 1970s brown linoleum that was partially covered in brown carpet, set off in yellow ochre squares. Over the years, and obviously long since the late Alamina Batley had been with us on this earth, Walter had disregarded the need to vacuum, or even *Wash 'N' Vac* the carpet covering the linoleum. It was bordering on the disgraceful! I immediately visualised Adam tearing it from the floor and heaving the sorry covering out of the kitchen window into an empty skip!

To help clear my head, I looked out of the long thin kitchen window towards the beautifully swaying trees outside as a way of distracting myself from the sorry situation inside the room. Below the window sat a small wooden table. It had a yellow formica top to it, the sort my grandma would have had in her kitchen. The one leaf was extended, with a little rusty hinge down the middle. The table was pushed up against the wall in the corner, trapping one of the straight-backed pine chairs in its place like a rose pinned to a trellis. Another matching chair stood opposite, patiently waiting for the ghost of Alamina to return.

Glancing up at the ceiling it appeared to be in reasonable condition, and I imagined with a fresh plaster coat and a whitewash, finished off with a deep cornice to match the lounge, it could be amazing. Maybe a ceiling rose with a crystal chandelier dropping down over an island unit to finish off! My heart was taking over again.

Looking around, it was plainly obvious that the kitchen units, being old and in dire need of updating, would all need to be replaced, but on the positive side, there was plenty of space for that, and a nice island unit in the middle of the room with a granite work surface. My vision was modern, light and practical.

Adam caught my eye and raised an eyebrow yet again. I could see he was thinking, *too old, too much work and too much money!*

I was thinking, *has great potential. Could be done* and *Wow!*

Next, we were led down the passageway and shown into the bathroom. Walter led the way and opened the door and stepped in, followed by Adam. I stayed just outside as I imagined it to be a small enclosed space.

Surprisingly as I poked my head round the bathroom door, I was amazed to find this was also a large room with a generous ceiling height, but again, the fixtures and fittings would have to be replaced. The only fitting in the room of a modern design was the heated towel rail. It was large, shiny and chrome and was obviously new. It looked so out of place, but it gave me the inspiration I needed to visualise the whole room as it might be in the future. A sparkling white, ceramic Jacuzzi bathtub, overhead power shower, matching vanity unit and a high Victorian style, chain-pulling toilet system, finished off with a hard wood, mahogany toilet seat. There was even room for a bidet, if required.

The floor was covered in linoleum yet again, this time cream in colour with a fine dark green marble effect wavy line design running through it. An old faded pink bathmat hung limply over the edge of the cast-iron bath, whose claw feet seemed implanted on the spongy floor like an overweight rhino stuck in a muddy swamp.

Hanging from the lofty ceiling was a single light bulb on the end of a cable. I guessed Walter was unable to reach such a monumental height to replace the shade that had previously adorned the exposed 40-watt bulb.

Walter turned round and waved his brown freckled hand in the direction of the door. 'Shall we move on to the bedrooms?' he volunteered.

As we ventured down the hallway, we passed a large airing cupboard that aroused my husband's curiosity, and he ground to a halt. 'Is this the boiler?' he said in a louder-than-necessary voice. Walter stopped in his tracks, turned round, retraced a few steps and opened the door with a creak. We peered into the gloomy space, spiders ran in every direction, hiding in every crevice or crack away from the light that now streamed into their quiet inconspicuous little world.

The copper boiler was wrapped in a lagging jacket made of a thick orange leathery foam, and a thin red, badly fitting insulating jacket was draped loosely over it. This was tied on with red-and-white twine. Adam winced!

'Bloody good boiler,' said Walter. 'Should see me out.'

Adam was not so sure and gave me a poke in the back. As I turned to look at him, he grimaced.

Walter pushed the door shut, allowing the clutter of spiders to breathe a sigh of relief and return to what spiders do in the dark.

Following Mr Walter Batley down the passageway, we came to the much-anticipated bedroom, one of two. My spirits rose as we entered the bright, sun-drenched spacious room; the sun had come out and its rays filtered through the long line of windows that stretched the full length of the inside wall. The adjoining wall was painted in satin magnolia and housed even more casement windows, giving a magnificent view from the large dark-framed four-poster bed. The tops of the line of chestnut trees that lined the drive could be glimpsed as they swayed in the breeze.

The room was overfilled with antique furniture, including a walnut dressing table complete with matching, free-standing oval vanity mirror, the glass a little frosted now with age. It stood against one wall, a matching stool tucked under the table, resting where the late Mrs Batley must have pushed it when she last sat down to brush her hair. Two bedside tables in mahogany wood, each with a drawer beset with light wooden marquetry inlay, graced either side of the four-poster bed, whose high canopy almost touched the ceiling.

Along one of the walls was the biggest wardrobe I had ever seen. The book, *The Lion, the Witch and the Wardrobe*, sprang into my mind. I wondered, if I opened the huge door and stepped in, whether there would be a winter wonderland on the other side. It was enormous!

Created in walnut, there were beautifully carved flowers running the entire length of each huge door, scrolls of intricate fretwork graced the full length of the top and bottom of the mammoth piece, and a full-length bevelled mirror fell between the two impressive doors. There was even an ornate brass lock set into each door with its own crafted key. It was the work of true craftsmanship from a bygone age, and it was sitting here in the room it had been designed for, probably from the time that Battlefields had been built. It had never been moved, probably because that would have been impossible once it had been assembled.

I imagined that it was still full of Alamina's clothing; perhaps an ankle-length mink fur coat was hanging in the wardrobe or a heavily sequinned flapper dress, complete with feather boa or maybe an elegant feathered hat. I wondered what sort of person Alamina had been and what she might have worn in that bygone era when folk dressed up to go to the theatre, dancing or to dinner.

Walter interrupted my thoughts when he commented, 'If you like the four-poster antique bed, I've been offered a handsome price already, but it's still open to the highest bidder, just in case you were interested.' That faded blue eye flickered in my direction once again.

Adam held his hands up in a defensive gesture and there was a long pause before he added, 'That's all right, we have our own king-sized bed that would fit in nicely, but thank you anyway.' He obviously didn't fancy hopping into Walter and Alamina's four-poster with the thought of sleeping in the same bed that Alamina may have taken her last breath.

Was Adam coming round to the idea of living at Battlefields or was he just being polite to Walter. I wasn't quite sure. This was going to need some soul-searching on both our parts as to whether we took on this monster of an undertaking or whether we walked away.

Time was not on our side – we needed to find a new home and pretty quickly!

'Now I must take you to the study, or second bedroom if you prefer to call it that. Come this way, please,' said Walter suddenly. We trailed behind him like two little mice quietly following a hungry pussycat along the passageway to the end room. Here we found an area that had been partially divided at the time when property owner and developer Mr Charlie Bennet had seen fit to literally split the spacious room down the middle with a plasterboard wall. What would have once been an imposing semicircular room commanding fantastic views across the countryside, a first-floor dining room or sitting room – ultimately the best outlook within the Battlefields mansion – had been heartlessly barricaded down the middle and divided up to create two halves of a semicircle. One half of this room belonged to number 3 Battlefields House and the second half belonged to next door – number 2. It was most odd, but as my Adam said later, 'It is what it is.'

The room would be fine for our youngest son to use as a study/bedroom but it was a shame it had been radically altered in this way.

And that was another thought to peruse – what would our youngest, Ben, make of this place? Would he open his mind and arms at the same time and think it was 'WICKED!' or would he think we had 'LOST OUR MARBLES,' a thought which more often than not had passed through his nineteen-year-old head when thinking of his parents.

'Well, you've seen the apartment, so I suppose you will want to see the cellar too.'

We agreed, not actually realising there was a cellar that came with number 3.

Walter led us down the cantilever stairway, locking up as we left the apartment. 'Can't be too careful,' he muttered as he slowly made his way down to the hallway, gripping on to the filigree ironwork of the banister to steady himself. At the bottom of the stairway, he pointed towards an arched opening next to the front door, which we had not noticed before. 'This way,' he said 'the basement is down here.'

A light drizzle had begun to fall outside and darkness came over the room as we followed Walter down stone steps into the cellar. As we descended, I held on to the col stone wall, feeling my way down. The dank smell rose from the depths to meet our nostrils and reminded me of a crypt that I had visited in France many years ago. Walter fumbled in the dark and found a light switch on the wall, which lit a low-voltage bulb that hung from an electric cable above our heads.

'Now this is yours if you buy the flat,' he said as if he was giving us a bag of gold coins. He held up a brass key that dangled on an old piece of string that was attached to a brown luggage label. I could only just make out the words written in faded black ink *No. 3.* I thought Walter was passing me the key, so I reached out my hand as if to take it from him, only to have him snatch the key, string and label back and clutch them to his chest. He turned away and fiddled with the lock and key. I turned to Adam in the gloomy darkness and shrugged in a non-committal way. Whatever was coming next?

Walter unlocked the misfitted, man-made, scratched paintless door and pushed it open to reveal a dark space that smelt like an underground catacomb where decaying bodies are left to rot. It was a sobering thought.

A dim light came on as Walter flicked a switch on the cobwebby, flaky stone wall, the smell of damp infiltrating my nostrils. I half expected to see a long-suffering skeleton chained to the back wall, or a torture rack waiting for its next victim, but the only thing in there was an old leather trunk, secured with a large padlock on the front.

Well! It wasn't a room to sit and do my cross-stitch in, or paint my toenails, or host an afternoon tea party in, but it would be useful for storing my pottery wheel and the large amount of stoneware clay I would be bringing with me (if we did make an offer, of course, and decide Battlefields was for us). With the addition of some shelving and a good supply of electricity it would be an ideal cavern to store my ceramic masterpieces that I hoped to create, putting my BA Honours Degree in 3D Design to eventual use. My mind was wandering again to the possibilities of the place.

As there was not much else to see in the gloomy darkness, apart from a variety of additional padlocked doors that stretched on into the cellar, red taped boxes with numbers written on the sides, a variety of ladders and garden equipment leaning back on the main arched wall, and a number of white sheeted furniture covers that hid chairs and stools, which had obviously come from someone's flat in the past, there was nothing of great interest.

After retracing our steps back up to the hallway and into the semi-darkness, where it was now overcast and raining hard, we thanked Mr Walter Batley. Shaking his bony hand, we told him we would get in touch with Rosie about the apartment as soon as possible.

'Don't leave it too long – it won't be on the market for much longer. I think you two would fit right in here nicely,' he said as he closed the big oak door behind us.

We walked out into the rain and jumped into the car.

Before Adam could say anything, I voiced my thoughts. 'It is very unusual . . . it has the potential to be quite a unique place to live . . . the garden is endless . . . we could take long summer evening walks from the doorstep . . . the views from the apartment are outstanding . . . we could, with some work, turn it into a little paradise for ourselves . . .' And finally, 'It's just a stone's throw from the golf course.'

Adam looked at me, astounded. 'YOU LIKE IT?' he said.

'I LOVE IT!' I laughed.

I think Battlefields House had grown on me as we wandered round its thick, historical, solid stone walls. I had fallen in love with the uniqueness of the place, its history and the location. It was a decision that 'we might live to regret,' my dear husband Adam said as we finally signed the papers to purchase number 3 Battlefields House

CHAPTER 3

MOVING OUT, MOVING IN

14th February soon came round. The previous few days had been spent packing the large cardboard boxes we had previously been given by the removal company. They were labelled, sealed and stacked ready to go. Our worldly belongings sitting inside, family clothes were lined up hanging on clothes rails as advised by the removal experts. 'No need to fold and stack, just hang on coat hangers and leave to them to us,' Marcus, the owner of the removal company, had insisted.

Our home looked like a Chinese laundry. Boxes of multicoloured socks, stacks of stripy boxer shorts and an array of coloured bras were waiting for an empty black sack, which our son was rummaging around looking for. Ben our youngest son, now at Bristol University, was in his first year of study. He had decided to live at home and commute to the University as it was only twenty miles travel, and it would save him a small fortune on student accommodation fees. As yet he hadn't actually seen Battlefields House, and didn't seem too concerned that it was an old Gothic building in the countryside. Once he had his degree and a safe, rewarding career to step into, he would be looking for a small place of his own anyway. So, he had already made up his mind that where his parents chose to live was fine with him.

I did ask him once or twice if he wanted to take a look at the property anytime – I was happy to take him out to view the building from the car park – but as with most nineteen- year-olds, he was unperturbed and would go with the flow!

'If you and Dad are happy, I'm happy too,' he said, after the third time of asking, so I wisely let it rest there.

At 8.50 a.m. on the morning we moved house I heard the removal van arrive, beeping its way backwards into the cul-de-sac. Looking out of the window, Adam called out 'They're here!'

I peered out of the same window as the van came to a halt. Phyllis's net curtains were already twitching opposite at number 2 Fairoaks,– she was not going to miss a thing. A burly man dressed in a green overall, or onesie as my niece called it, climbed out of the driver's side and jumped down heavily on to the pavement. He did not look fit enough to be a removal man. Out of the passenger side two others alighted. The first was a youth, ginger-headed and looking like he could do with a good Sunday roast inside him. He was tall and lanky, like a thin willow tree that would snap in half at the slightest puff of wind. I wondered how he was going to cope with all the stairs leading up to the apartment. There were at least twenty stone steps to negotiate on a spiralling staircase! There was a three-seater sofa, armchairs, a king-sized bed frame and a large dining table and chairs, a kitchen table, a heavy mirrored dressing table and that was just the start.

The second youth was a young girl, attired in matching green overalls, a large pair of Dr Martin boots and tattoos covering most of her exposed skin. Her dark hair was tied back in a short ponytail that stuck through the back of her black cap like the rear end of a saddled horse in a stable.

The three musketeers walked up the path towards the front door, which was already open and welcoming.

Stepping inside the hallway the older man introduced himself as Seamus promptly shook my husband's hand vigorously. 'Any chance of a brew?' he asked with a cheeky grin as he turned and looked me in the eye. I explained that everything had been packed away, the pot and the kettle were in a box somewhere, and I was not too keen to rummage through all the crockery trying to lay my hands on a couple of mugs and a teapot at the very moment of our impending departure. He looked a little forlorn and scratched his head. 'We've been on the road for an hour already,' he said. 'We usually have a cuppa before we load up.' The other two nodded their heads in agreement.

What could I do? Reluctantly I went into the kitchen to locate the box marked in large, black capital letters KETTLE. I split the Sellotape sealing the box with a pair of scissors and rummaged through the scrunched-up newspaper, pulling out the kettle, teapot and three mugs that had been carefully stored ready for our arrival at Battlefields House. Next, I located the cool box that held all the food items that needed to be kept cool in transit. The milk was produced and I set everything back on the worktop and put the kettle on to boil. Ten minutes later the tea had been drunk and the satisfied threesome started to carry and load our precious cargo on to the van. Happy puppies!

Five hours later everything from Fairoaks had been removed and was now loaded in the big green removal lorry. Just at that moment Phyllis popped her head round the front door. 'I couldn't let you leave without bringing over a little house-warming present,' she said as she handed me a little brown bag. 'Open it when you get to your new home, and don't forget to come and visit when you have time, otherwise I'll be on the phone to you!'

I gave her a huge hug and told her I would miss her, but would give her a ring in a day or two to let her know how we were settling in. She wiped a little tear with her Kleenex and scuttled off back to number two, blowing her nose with a little sniff as she crossed the road.

We packed the few remaining items that were left into the back of the car: our son's guitar, a multipack of unopened toilet rolls and a box of wooden chess pieces that I had picked up on a trip to a Turkish bazaar in Istanbul on our last holiday. We stepped back into our house for the last time with our youngest son Ben, who was helping with the move.

'Well,' Adam said, 'this is it. Say goodbye to Fairoaks.

We all took a last look round and even our son felt a little sentimental about leaving his home. It was nice to see how attached he had become to the family home he had spent the last nineteen years growing up in.

Ten minutes later we climbed into the car with a view to dropping the keys off at the local estate agent's and bid a final farewell to our lovely family home.

The removal van had gone on ahead, so it was just a matter of following on in our own time. We wound our way along the country lanes, passing fields, where ponies galloped and sheep munched on the green tufts of grass, and continued on our journey towards Battlefields House.

My spirits rose as the view opened out and the sun came from behind a bank of cloud, bathing the countryside in a golden hue. Ben asked how far we had to go, and I assured him it was not far. We drove another hour or so, and finally drew up next to the same green sign we had spotted before.

BATTLEFIELDS HOUSE
PRIVATE DRIVE

'Here we are!' I said excitedly.

We turned into the lane that took us down the meandering drive to the car park. Ben glimpsed the Gothic building through the trees for the first time. 'You never said it was a castle!' he exclaimed. I had not thought of Battlefields as a castle before, but I guess to a nineteen-year-old, it could be seen as such. When we had first viewed the apartment, I had come away with a rose-tinted view of what the place could eventually look like – with a lot of tender loving care and an upgrade in just about every room. A coat of light Heritage paint to cover the nicotine-coloured walls, newly plastered ceilings, a long stretch of ornate plaster cornice and matching dado rails to break up the high walls in the bedroom, ceiling to floor Barmer fabric Buttercup yellow, patterned with climbing vines and foliage on a yellow background, would befit the endless windows and finally plush carpet throughout, oh and a scattering of thick colourful rugs and cushions to add interest to the lounge and bedrooms. I had it all planned out and had been visualising and mulling over my ideas for the past few weeks.

Now in stark reality we were here and Battlefields lay before us. Suddenly as we sat peering up at the grey lichen-covered stonework of the façade from our little car, it became a daunting prospect, a huge amount of hard work and an even bigger commitment to the financial side to the project.

My thoughts were brought to an abrupt end when I realised the removal van was nowhere in sight, and Rosie was not here either and we didn't have a key to get into the building.

Adam assured me the lorry would be along soon, and Rosie had assured him that she would bring along the keys to number three as soon as she heard from Walter, so we patiently waited . . .

Twenty minutes passed and we were still wondering where the van was, when a little yellow Fiat came speeding down the drive. It drew up next to us, causing a little cloud of dust to rise from its Dunlop tyres and Rosie jumped out, a little red in the face and a little flustered.

'Sorry I'm a bit behind – Walter couldn't find the Chubb key to the front door, but I've got it now, so no worries,' she said, slightly embarrassed.

She handed a bunch of keys over to Adam and we thanked her for all the help in securing the sale. She jumped back in her car after wishing us good luck and disappeared like a rat up a drainpipe before we could ask her any questions about the keys.

Ben, who had been extremely quiet for the whole time we had been in the car park, suddenly looked up and said, 'Do you think it's haunted?'

'Well, if it is, I'm sure the ghost will manifest itself in good time,' Adam teased.

Ben's eyebrows knitted together in a McKenzie frown, causing a long dark monobrow to stretch across his forehead – a McKenzie trait when a worrying or threatening situation has occurred. Just at that moment the removal van with 'We Like to Move It' emblazoned on the side came into view, banishing all thoughts of ghouls and ghosts out of Ben's head, at least for now.

The three musketeers, Athos, Porthos and Aramis, jumped down from the cab of the lorry, the older man apologising for the delay in their arrival, stating that they had passed a roadside café en route to their destination. Predicting that there would be a long day ahead, they had unanimously decided to pull over and have a brew and a bacon butty. What could I say? He could have lied and blamed the delay on a puncture or an animal death on the road or an attack by a swarm of killer bees! But no, he had a craving for a bacon butty and our move could wait!

The large green doors at the back of the lorry were unlocked and the tailgate lowered ready for the great unloading ceremony. At that moment the big oak front door opened and a head topped with brown curly hair poked out. 'You must be the McKinseys,' the head stated in an accent I did not recognise.

Adam stepped forward, stretching out his hand. '*McKenzies*,' he corrected in the most friendly of manners.

'Oh, sorry,' the curly-headed neighbour said apologetically. 'Batley said you were the McKinseys, but old Walter was pretty hard of hearing, you know. He's better off in the care home his daughter found for him – he won't be so isolated and lonely. Bloody good care home I understand. Mind you, it's not surprising he can afford it, I heard he had an auctioneer in to value his antiques – got a small fortune and even sold his Delftware to a London auction house.'

Adam looked at me, but didn't have the audacity to ask how much he got for them.

I took the keys out of Adam's hand while he stood pontificating over the lost treasures of Walter Batley's Delftware.

The friendly neighbour introduced himself as Felix Jones from number eight, apparently. He lived there with his wife. The basement flat, as we found out later, was Battlefields' main cellar.

It was not until six months later and a prearranged visit to see Felix and his wife Madalyn that I got to see their underground apartment. An actual wine cellar had become their home. With no windows, stone arched walls at every turn and only just enough head-room to stand up in, I was amazed that two such friendly sweet folk could reside in such an unusually cramped abode. They appeared to be quite happy there, but over the years we did notice they spent an awful lot of time in the garden, where they had a permanent wrought-iron table and chair at the top of the cellar steps, allowing them to enjoy *petit déjeuner* in the open air, even in the middle of winter. Ben once noted that they always seemed to have red noses like the gnome on Phyllis's front lawn.

Felix left us with a 'Catch you later when you have settled in.'

If all our neighbours turn out to be as nice as Felix, we would feel very welcome here, I thought positively.

The trip up the cantilever staircase was a huge blow for the removal team. The first box was carried up by the boss, but being a little overweight, he struggled to reach the tenth stair, giving a little puff of air and a wheeze as he passed me on the stairway. The youth who was called Riff, seemed to float up and down the steps with no trouble at all, hardly breaking into a sweat as he whistled his way up and down, carrying various pieces of furniture and bric-a-brac.

I was organising where the boxes should go, which rooms

certain items needed to be moved into or out of, when suddenly my attention was caught by Adam laughing out loud. He called Ben and me into the lounge, where he pointed to the wall over the fireplace. Above the mantelpiece hung the oil painting of the youth and his dog, peering out from the picture, eyeing us hauntingly.

'I can't believe Walter left that here,' I gasped.

'Perhaps it comes with the territory. You know – you buy the place and the creepy-looking youth comes with it,' laughed Adam, glancing at the mortified Ben.

Ben looked at the eerie portrait, stepping closer. 'God, it looks like me when I was that age,' he stuttered in disbelief.

I reached up and took the painting down off the wall, seeing the distress it was causing Ben and tucked it behind the newly positioned settee, saying it didn't look anything like him, although I was a bit taken back at the likeness to Ben.

(It stayed hidden and out of sight until many years later when our little niece found it and pulled it out, covered in cobwebs. She gave the painting a hug and called him *Gallee*. She loved the image and every time she came to visit, she would ask where *Gallee* was, and I had to pull the hidden ghostly painting out from behind the settee. So eventually we dusted it off and put it back on the wall, much to Ben's dismay and Adam's amusement, where it stayed until the day we left Battlefields House.)

In the meantime, the removal guys and gal were heaving the endless number of boxes up the stairway, the older of them cussing blindly every time he set foot in the apartment. He seemed to grow grumpier by the box! Eventually he disappeared and only the flitty youth and the young tattooed prima donna continued to enter the premises. I eventually saw him from the turret window having a crafty cigarette behind the garage wall.

Eventually there was one item of concern left in the removal van – the gigantic American fridge-freezer. I had woken up in the middle of the night the previous week with a nightmare: the fridge-freezer had been tumbling down the cantilever stairway with Walter Batley bounding after it shouting 'Make way! Make way!'

It had been so real that I woke Adam up and told him about it. He assured me it could not have been Walter, as he really couldn't bound down the stairs and told me to go back to sleep. So positively factual, but he was right, Walter could not possibly have bounded anywhere, especially down the stairs. I turned over and after several minutes of berating myself for being so idiotic I did go back to sleep.

The head of the removal threesome suggested we congregate downstairs at the back of the van with a view to discussing the massive undertaking now about to unfold. A battle plan was put into action, the tailgate was lowered yet again and the fridge-freezer was leant backwards into a semi-reclining position, which was no mean undertaking in itself. With a sort of shuffle, shoulder heave-ho approach, the American giant was manoeuvred on to a set of low trolleys, like lifting a sedated elephant on to a flatbed. The trolleys were slowly wheeled to the steps of Battlefields, where it took the three of them to lift and roll the heavy beast up and over the steps. The big single oak door was too narrow to get the mighty freezer through, so the second door had to be prised open and hooked back out of harm's way.

Adam, myself and Ben stood back admiring the professional

removers wincing, groaning and blaspheming as they made their cautious way to the bottom of the stairs.

'Now what?' said the spotty youth.

'We lift it; I'll go ahead and guide you up,' said Seamus. 'You two get behind and lift when I say.' There was a slight pause. 'Got it?'

'Yes, boss,' came the reply in unison from the other two.

It was surreal to watch as the three of them lifted, humped and cajoled the heavy inanimate object step by painful step up and up the cantilevered stairway. I was wondering if the weight of the object would cause the stone stairway to collapse under the weight, sending the three of them and the fridge-freezer crashing down into the hallway, and then on down into the basement!

At one point I held my breath as the heavy aluminium rectangle tottered on the top step of the stairway, then lurched forward a foot before regaining its balance, like a man on a unicycle. It was a sight to behold. Finally, the great beast was manhandled into position within the kitchen recess, where it fitted perfectly. We all breathed a sigh of relief!

The skies were darkening as the three furniture removers finally made their weary way down the stairs for the last time. After thanking them and promising to return their boxes as soon as they had been emptied of all their contents, we closed the apartment door and breathed a sigh of relief, yet again for the last time that day.

We fell into our unmade bed that night completely exhausted and, pulling the quilt up round us, we lay our tired heads on pillowcase-less pillows and fell asleep in our new home.

CHAPTER 4

THE MANAGEMENT COMMITTEE MEETING

The next morning, we awoke to bright sunshine, having no curtains at the windows, Walter having taken every last curtain ring, light bulb and even the toilet roll from the bathroom with him. I padded to the kitchen to make Adam a cup of tea when I saw a white envelope mysteriously appear under the front door. I picked it up and put it on the tray alongside the two mugs on my way back to the bedroom.

The letter contained an invitation to the next Battlefields management committee meeting to be held on 18 February at number 1 on the top floor of the building. The minutes of the last meeting were laid out and the agenda for the next meeting followed.

AGENDA

1. New Chairman Appointee
2. Garden Maintenance Contract
3. Roof Project
4. Annual Fundraising

5. Chestnut Concern
6. Carpet Replacement
7. Any Other Business

The meeting was to be held in Michael and Helen's apartment, number 1, and drinks and canapés would be served prior to the meeting, which would start at seven p.m.

Please be prompt, it said at the bottom of the invitation.

I thought this would be a good opportunity to meet all the residents at once, and Adam was interested in finding out how the management committee members ran the Battlefields empire. We were both looking forward to the evening.

The 18 February came round and after arriving home from work Adam quickly changed into jeans and a polo shirt and ate his tea just in time to prepare for the meeting. He had a few questions to ask the chairman about the financial side of the running of Battlefields House and estate. We had a few concerns about the stair carpet and the roof over our kitchen, which we understood from Walter was due for re-felting.

This would be the first time we would be meeting most of the residents who lived alongside us in this unusual house in the countryside, and we wanted to give a good impression of ourselves, as well as get to know the people around us. Up until now we had only met Felix from the cellar, and the Italian Francesco from number seven, whom we had previously bumped into in the car park the day before. He had seemed pleasant enough, having shaken hands with us both, and passed the time enquiring where we had lived before our move and why we had chosen Battlefields to make our home. Apparently,

Francesco was treasurer on the committee and would therefore be the person responsible for financial decisions and inhouse spending at Battlefields House.

At ten to seven we climbed the stairway, commenting negatively to each other on the state of the carpet, as we made our way round and up the spiralling staircase to number 1. After ringing the doorbell, we heard a clicking of heels on the tiled floor on the other side of the door, a slight pause, a sigh and then the door opened.

'Welcome, new neighbours, I'm Helen, Michael's wife,' said a slim attractive thirty-something-year-old, dark-haired lady. The little pink mule slippers she was wearing had been the cause of the clickety-click on the tiles. Her beautifully manicured toenails were painted a bright red to match her very long polished fingernails, which in turn matched her ruby-red lipstick. She smiled and took us through to the lounge-diner.

The first thing I noticed was the number of framed certificates hanging on the lounge wall, regimented lines of black A1 plastic frames containing official documents with subjects Michael had obviously studied in his adult life. They appeared, on closer inspection, to be diplomas and certificates in the subjects of anxiety, mindfulness and psychology. As I was just about to comment on the certificate in psychology, Michael popped his head round the kitchen door and came out with a tray of white wine and several orange juices. Helen reappeared behind Michael with a plate of canapés that consisted of a selection of Ritz crackers with a dollop of Philadelphia cheese squirted on the top, rounded off with a pink prawn sitting slightly erect on top of the cream cheese.

Offering us a drink, Michael invited us over to a ring of

assorted chairs where four guests had already taken their seats. Felix was sitting next to Madalyn Jones, who we assumed to be his wife, and opposite were a couple I had not seen before. They soon became known to us as Jeremy and Jessica, or JJ, the couple from number six, who turned out to be the brother of Felix the cellar resident.

There was a loud knock on the door and two more people were ushered into the room. These were the treasurer Francesco and his long-standing wife Lena Romano. Francesco was a typical Italian, dark-haired, tanned complexion, very hairy arms and thick black eyebrows; Lena was quite the opposite – white-haired, pale complexion and of German descent. She spoke in a curt, direct manner; he with continental expressive hand gestures.

After making small talk for a few minutes, as we got to know our new neighbours a little, Michael, who had temporarily taken over as chairman from the now-absent Walter Batley, tapped his glass with a spoon and called us all to order, as the bride's father might do at his daughter's wedding.

The last to arrive just as Michael was tapping his glass, was a young man by the name of Daniel from number four. He made excuses for his wife not attending and sat on the rocking chair next to the window, where he proceeded to rock gently back and forth. He gave the impression that he didn't really want to be at the meeting – I suspected his wife had sent him in her place and had found something a little more interesting to do.

Daniel and Felicity had their rooms on the ground floor overlooking the front lawn. They had, on moving in several years ago, decided that the most impressive room with the most spectacular views from the apartment was to be their bedroom, even though the interior of the room could be viewed directly from the lawns outside, allowing anyone with an ounce of curiosity to peek in as they went by. The huge full-length windows allowed full visual access to their high-ceilinged, very comfortable boudoir. It so happened on more than one occasion in the years to come, when out enjoying the garden, I had unwittingly observed a white naked body streaking from one room to another, like a flash of bright lightning on a dark winter's night.

Apparently, it had been raised in a previous management meeting by a resident, whose mother-in-law had got the shock of her life when she stood up from her deckchair in the garden one sunny afternoon and was confronted by Daniel and Felicity cavorting under the eiderdown in their ground-floor bedroom. She had registered a complaint to the Management company chairman, who had in turn raised the misdemeanour with Daniel and Felicity, who were amused and really did not see the problem, but promised to close their curtains if a romantic moment arose again on a Sunday afternoon. The subject had not been mentioned since, or so Felix informed me later.

Chairman Michael cleared his throat and the meeting began.

An introduction was made on our behalf to all the residents, and apologies were offered for the absentees. The couple from number five, the Mathers, were absent since they lived in South Africa most of the time, and Battlefields House was their retirement home for the future. They rarely came over to England and apparently Lena kept an eye on their apartment, ventilating the property when necessary, picking up any mail and checking for vermin.

The mysterious lady from number two, by the surname of Whipsnake according to her name on the front-door bell, was missing too. I had only seen her from a distance when she stepped out of a rather striking bronze-coloured Bentley late the previous evening. She had been accompanied by a very smartly dressed gentleman, and they had come into Battlefields and had obviously gone to her apartment. Mysteriously the next morning the smartly dressed man and the striking Bentley were nowhere to be seen.

The minutes of the last meeting were read out and the items on the agenda were announced by Michael.

'Item one on the agenda, appointment of a new chairperson,' said Michael. 'In the absence of Walter, I have temporarily taken on the role of Chairman of Battlefields' Management Company and we now need to appoint a new chairman to take on this important role; can we have any nominees, please?'

There was a long embarrassing silence. Daniel stopped rocking back and forth, avoiding everyone's gaze and looked out of the window. Felix and Madalyn solemnly shook their heads and looked at Jeremy and Jessica, hoping that they might step forward and offer to take up the position. Francesco stood up and discounted himself but offered to remain as treasurer for the indefinite future, so that only left Adam and myself. All eyes in the room suddenly came to rest on Adam!

'Would you consider taking on the position?' asked Michael. Well, poor Adam was stuck between a rock and a hard place. What could he say?

'I really appreciate you asking, but we are new to Battlefields, and I think you should have someone who has resided here a little longer and knows what's what,' he said defensively.

Francesco rubbed his stubbly chin and reminded Adam that he had been running an American business for over ten years and becoming chairman was relatively easy here at Battlefields. It was in name only really, the most time-consuming job being treasurer, which he was happy to continue to be.

Where he had obtained his information about Adam's background and position we never found out, we could only assume he had looked him up on the internet.

Michael assured Adam that there would be plenty of help on offer if Adam wanted advice or information on the running of Battlefields House. Francesco thought Adam would fit in nicely to the position as he had so much experience in running a company.

Before Adam could refuse or argue his point further, the motion was passed and seconded and the next item on the agenda was raised.

ITEM 2
RENEWAL OF THE GARDEN MAINTENANCE CONTRACT.

It apparently had been raised on several occasions in the past that residents were not happy with the contractors who maintained the extensive lawns around the building. Grass clippings, the nettle bank and grass verges were of concern, especially by the Joneses at number six. They had previously offered to purchase the equipment necessary to take on the contract themselves in return for not paying their share of the building maintenance cost every month. Their offer had been denied several times in the past as it was thought that the job required professional intervention. Once again, the Joneses put their case that it made perfect sense that living at Battlefields, which was their home, they had a vested interest in maintaining the lawns to a high standard and to the residents' satisfaction. The machinery, which included a high-spec sit-on lawnmower, trailer and various other pieces of equipment, would be purchased, maintained and replaced, if necessary, all at their own expense. The offer would also do away with the existing garden contract and the company that was underperforming.

I thought this was a great idea and so did Adam, as he secretly hoped he might be invited to help with the sit-on mower side of things.

Unfortunately, the motion was denied after a management committee vote and J and J's proposition was turned down on the grounds that everyone thought Jeremy and Jessica wanted to be let off the maintenance monthly fee that we all contributed to. This was required for the upkeep of the building – they wanted to volunteer their services for free instead of paying into the maintenance fund.

It made sense to us to give the new contract a trial run, allowing J and J at least six months of maintaining the garden. But it was refused, leaving Jeremy and Jessica rather annoyed that their plans had not been accepted yet again!

Francesco had insisted that he could find a local gardening outfit that would be cheaper than the price being paid now; he, being financial treasurer, would look into it further, and it was left like that.

'Moving on to item three on the agenda,' Michael said quickly, cutting out any further verbal disagreements and bad feeling on the subject.

ROOFING PROJECT NUMBER 3

This was a concern for us, as Walter had stated that money had been set aside in the finances for new felting over our kitchen roof, which was due to be replaced before the winter of this year. This was a topic that we were very interested in as it involved our apartment and us.

The motion had already been passed in the last financial committee meeting and the go-ahead given, but nobody had set the roof re-felting wheels in motion, so nothing had been organised yet. This we were concerned about and wondered why this project had not progressed, as it had been given the go-ahead at least twice in the last two meetings and was discussed at least a year ago prior to our arrival. We found out later that Walter had put the whole project on hold as he was planning to move out and did not want the upheaval or problems the project might show up.

Francesco made muttered apologies and tried to find excuses for the oversight. He promised to get on it right away and would organise two quotes from reliable roofing contractors, but he warned it would be expensive because Battlefields was a listed building and therefore everything connected with maintenance was at a premium price. 'We only have so much in the pot,' he mumbled under his garlicky infused breath.

We felt quite relieved that the project would now ensue and we would sleep well in the knowledge that Francesco was on the roofing case and we trusted he would be true to his word, or so we thought.

After a short coffee break and a stretch of our legs, the meeting had taken two hours already to get through just half of the topics on the agenda. We sat in our chosen seats and the second round of the meeting began.

ITEM 4
ANNUAL FUNDRAISING

Jessica was still smouldering from her earlier defeat over the gardening contract but came up with an idea to raise money towards the stone masonry funding. Apparently, the granite stonework that Battlefields was originally built from was gradually crumbling in certain areas and urgent restoration was needed, especially on the front façade. Funding over the years had been held back by Walter Batley on several occasions, as the financial situation at the house had been quite insufficient to warrant spending large sums of money, he had said.

Jessica thought an open garden day at Battlefields might be an excellent fundraising event. The idea would be to sell tickets locally to a limited number of people, perhaps a hundred, and the residents would lay on events in the garden. It could be organised for the coming summer – games and a bring-your-own picnic afternoon could raise perhaps a thousand pounds, if not more. She went on to explain that she had given it some thought and if we could find somewhere for cars to park locally it could be a fun event and profitable at the same time. She finished her prepared speech with a resigned-to-fail look on her face. She had already braced herself for the fact that she might not convince the committee to back her idea.

I felt a little sorry for her – after all, I thought it was a splendid idea.

Adam and I felt the same and we wholeheartedly climbed on board the fundraising Battlefields bus. We discussed the type of ideas that would be suitable: perhaps a children's game of Hunt for the Scarecrow. Felix suggested making a pair of old-fashioned stocks and he would volunteer to be wet-sponged for fifty pence a throw. I suggested making cupcakes to sell and home-made lemonade. There could be a bric-a-brac table with any odd items surplus to requirements donated by residents.

The ideas suddenly started to spew forth; even Lena joined in, saying that she would organise an apple-bobbing barrel, using the apples from the small orchard in the grounds. Madalyn suggested hiring someone to play music, which prompted the idea from Michael to search out an old gramophone in his attic that had belonged to his grandfather. He even had some old vinyl records that he would dust off. It was all very exciting.

The motion was passed and everyone was enthusiastic that this could be achieved with a lot of thought and planning. A date for July was agreed and I volunteered to co-ordinate the event along with Madalyn, who was just as enthusiastic as myself. After all, we needed to raise some serious funding to maintain the exterior of Battlefields House and stop it from crumbling to the ground. A sobering thought, as this was our home now and we felt we had a responsibility to preserve and restore the little kingdom that surrounded us all.

Michael moved us on to item number five. Time was ticking

away and it was now 9.30 and we still had another three items to get through, Adam was getting a little fidgety and wanting his nightcap of hot chocolate and two ginger biscuits, but he sat and listened to all the discussions intently. I knew he had made the decision to move here to Battlefields for me and he still needed to be convinced deep down that the decision was the right one and we had not taken on 'a minefield', as he put it!

ITEM 5
THE CHESTNUT CONCERN

Well, according to the Joneses, those living at number 6 not number 4, the chestnut tree at the bottom of the drive was causing them a modicum of concern. Every autumn for the past three years it had dropped its leaves far too early. They insisted something was amiss and had done various searches on the internet and researched the diseases and problems that could affect chestnut trees. Francesco took a lot of convincing that there was a real problem and was reluctant to take matters further due to the expense of calling out an expert in these matters. 'Anyway,' he stated a little forcefully, 'the trees have been here for centuries and will probably see me out.' This was not very helpful and obviously annoyed Jessica for the second time this evening.

Adam stepped in before things got out of hand and offered to contact an old friend of his who just happened to be a tree surgeon. Charlie Samplar was an acquaintance of Adam's who played cricket with the over-fifties Somerset team, whom Adam had also played for throughout the summer months. He assured the management committee and Francesco particularly, that

Charlie would be the perfect person to offer advice on this subject and would do it as a personal favour to Adam.

This idea was welcomed by Francesco as there would be no financial outgoings, but I was unsure whether Francesco would agree to spend the finances if there turned out to be a problem. He held on to the Battlefields purse strings very tightly.

Adam was already taking charge of the meeting despite his reluctance to be nominated. He was a natural choice and would use his negotiating skills to bring the management committee members to order and get things done. It was obvious to us both that this was called for, as not much had been achieved while Walter Batley had been chairman of the committee over the last ten years. So, Adam made a note on his pad to contact Charlie as soon as possible.

ITEM 6
THE REPLACEMENT OF THE STAIR CARPET

Another topic that had been raised but nothing achieved, was the much-needed replacement of the worn and faded stair carpet that ran like a muddy meandering river from the hallway, past our apartment and on up to Michael and Helen's apartment at the top of the building. It had been discussed several times in the past but no decision had been agreed upon as to who would undertake the project and get estimates, samples and organise the fitting of new carpet. As it affected apartments one, two and three the most, the residents in the other apartments were reluctant to get involved as they never used the stairway so were not interested in getting the project underway.

All the residents had agreed that the carpet was to be replaced, even Francesco had reserved funding over the last two years for the project, but unfortunately it had been put on the back burner while Walter was chairman and nobody had given it much thought since.

Well, this provided us with the opportunity to do something about it. I volunteered to get estimates for the replacement. I would ring around and spend some time at various carpet stores and bring samples of colour, texture and quality back for the residents who were interested, then we could proceed and make this exciting venture happen. Francesco would be informed about costing for the project and any final decisions would be announced at the next meeting, which was to be held a month from that day.

'Excellent,' said Michael. 'Is there any other business?'

It was 10.30 p.m. now and everyone was thinking about bed, but then Michael as acting chairman remembered that he had not officially welcomed Adam as chairman and proceeded to thank him for taking the job over. He got up from his chair, disappeared behind the settee and picked up a large cardboard box with the words 'MGM NOTES AND MINUTES' written on the side in big black letters. He handed the box to Adam and asked him if he would like to take charge of the papers relating to all the meeting minutes over the past ten years, and then asked if we would be holding the meeting at our apartment next month.

What could Adam say but 'Of course.' We walked out of number 1 feeling slightly uneasy about the whole situation we found ourselves in.

Several days later and up to our ears in stripping age-old anaglypta from the passageway walls, a small brown envelope was pushed under the front door. I quickly peeped through the spyhole halfway up the door but the view through the fish-eye lens seemed to be focused in the upward direction of the stairway, so you could see who was going up, but not who had gone down the stairs. It was most annoying.

Tearing the envelope open with my finger I read out loud, enabling Adam to hear first- hand the contents of the note. It was from Francesco. It read:

Dear Residents

I have taken it upon myself to obtain several quotes from local gardening contractors for the upkeep of the lawns here at Battlefields.

One company in particular has recently started a new business and after speaking directly to the company owner he has agreed to commence lawn-cutting on a fortnightly basis at a very competitive rate. Therefore, with due notice, I have terminated the present contract with Daniel and Son, our present contractor, and have signed a new contract for two years with Green Fingers Garden Maintenance, who will commence next Wednesday. The contractor, Dennis, has agreed to cut all the lawns, disposing of the grass cuttings in the wooded area behind the garages. He also agreed to cut the nettle-bank twice a year after in-depth negotiations with myself, and as a favour for getting his first big contract.

'That will really annoy Jessica,' Adam warned. 'I have the feeling Francesco and Jessica haven't seen eye to eye over several things that have happened in the past. I agreed with you that the contract should have gone to Jeremy and Jessica it made good sense.'

We continued cracking off the large pieces of brittle wallpaper. It came off the wall like dried cowpats and fell to the floor like shards of roof slate falling off an old cottage.

'Well, we will see what this new outfit is like, but as they made me chairman, I will have more input in making decisions in the future and if the contractors don't step up to the mark, they will have me to contend with.'

Fighting talk! I thought to myself.

CHAPTER 5

THE McKENZIE GOLF CUP

Over that week we busied ourselves in the apartment, rubbing down paintwork, ripping up carpet and cleaning windows, giving us a free weekend to enjoy the garden and surrounding woodland, and the time to explore the lovely countryside around us. Adam was itching to have a round of golf at the nearby golf club so had phoned our eldest son Thomas, who was free on Saturdays, and suggested a round. He planned to pick him up and his clubs and treat him to an afternoon out.

I was itching to get down to the greenhouse, which I had noticed when we arrived at Battlefields. It was situated just a short stretch from the garages, down the embankment and through the trees. It was a beautiful little spot sitting in dappled shade surrounded by meadow grass and flowers. It was so pretty.

The views through the fencing alongside were over the countryside where the ponies from nearby farms were grazing. The greenhouse was reached by a few little steps and was almost out of sight of the main house.

As I approached, I noticed Jessica bending over at a most embarrassing angle, with her head almost between her legs, deep in thought with her back to the greenhouse door.

I cleared my voice to enlighten her to my presence and she turned round a little too quickly and fell off the up-turned bucket she was sitting on.

'Sorry to disturb you', I said. 'I didn't realise there was anyone down here.'

Jessica burst out laughing! 'Come on down,' she said, standing up and brushing the dirt from her buttocks. 'I was miles away, thinking of this year's planting and trying to sort out all these bulbs I was planning to plant out on the embankment in the Spring'

Scattered all round her feet were hundreds of last year's bulbs that she had dried out all through the winter and was now sorting the good healthy ones from the few that had become soft or had mildew round the roots. I was pleased to help and pulled out a second upturned bucket to assist her.

We spent a nice few hours together, also cleaning out the terracotta pots with hot soapy water that were stored behind the glasshouse, generally cleared away anything not required and gave the whole place inside and out a thorough clean.

She told me of the plans she had for the wooded area and said it would be nice to have some help, as none of the other residents really bothered with the greenhouse and rarely came down to the area at all. She felt it was a shame because, even though the glasshouse was quite ancient, it had a quality about it that only time can give. A few panes were cracked and the wind blew through the glass framework making a noise like a toothless fairy playing a set of bagpipes. In addition to that, the old bench where she potted up plants had seen better days, leaning at an angle that at any moment might give up the ghost and gently fold in on itself.

Jessica had painstakingly brought on a hundred cuttings each year to plant into the garden the following season – sweet-smelling lavender, thyme and rosemary, and this was what had made it the charming little hideaway it had become for her, and she was willing for me to join her and help. I was honoured to be asked and thanked her for inviting me to be a part of this little venture.

She complained that Francesco never felt the improvement of the gardens round the house were a necessity and that the finances would be better spent elsewhere.

Having lived at Battlefields for fourteen years she had helped the gardens flourish and quietly went about improving areas that she felt needed a little TLC. Francesco never seemed to notice the improvements, or if he did he never mentioned it. Perhaps he feared if he made a complimentary comment, it might inspire Jessica to do more, and if she did more, she might require a monetary reimbursement.

She felt that as long as she did not seek financial support from the Battlefields' coffers for any plants, shrubs or bulbs she purchased, Francesco would keep his distance and leave her alone to carry on, as she had done so for the whole time she and Jeremy had been living there. Well, now I was here to help and we would make a formidable twosome and stand up to Francesco and his indifferent and tight-fisted approach.

We sat and enjoyed a coffee from her flask and a piece of home-made coconut and cherry cake she had freshly baked that morning. Life was looking up!

When Adam finally returned, he was pleased to hear of my afternoon exploits and even accepted graciously that our eldest son, Thomas, had beaten him yet again at golf. He could never quite take the McKenzie Cup at the end of the year and put it on our mantelpiece.

The McKenzie Cup had been a family golf tradition played once a year between Adam, Thomas, Ben and their Uncle Duncan, Adam's younger brother. I had purchased a little trophy in the form of a silver cup on a wooden plinth and had it engraved with the family name. I presented it at the end of the annual golf round to the winner and took a photograph of the presentation of the cup. That was always after we had all indulged in a chicken burger and chips in the golf club restaurant, the losers having to pay for the meal.

It was a great event and I was always invited to drive the golf buggy, taking pictures and little videos of them all in motion. Good and bad shots, bunker disasters and divot repairs were all included. It provided some great entertainment value on a cold winter's evening and a family tradition at Christmas when we all got together.

We were settling in very nicely at Battlefields; it seemed a quiet place to live. In among the trees we were quite isolated from all the hustle and bustle of city life in Bath just eight miles away. Yet things were to get interesting as time went on and not so idyllic or quiet!

The weekend came to an end and Adam went back to work. I continued to strip the wallpaper, scrub the walls with sugar soap and hot water, cleaning off years of discoloured grime from the paintwork and generally cleaned the whole apartment.

CHAPTER 6

GREEN FINGERS

On Monday morning Adam was up early to go to work. As he opened the front door and trotted down the stairway he called back, 'Don't forget the new garden contractors are coming today to cut the lawns. See if you could put a word in for me and offer my help next time they call – I would love to sit on their mower just once and cut perfectly straight stripes the length of the lawn.'

I laughed at the thought of Adam on a mower and promised if I saw them, I would do just that!

I took my coffee into the lounge where bare walls and dust-streaked windows without curtains greeted me, and sat in the little turret window looking out over the lawn. It was going to be a fine day; there was blue sky and fluffy white cumulonimbus clouds on the horizon, the trees were still and the sun was rising in the sky. All was well with the world, or so I thought!

As I sat there, I saw Francesco walk out of the main front door. He was on his mobile phone and even though I could not quite hear his words, I could see he was not a happy bunny. He was gesturing with his free hand and walking in circles round the car park.

I wondered what had upset him so much. I was to find out later that the garden contractors had cancelled the date they were supposed to start due to a mower malfunction. They assured Francesco they would come the following day at nine o'clock as had been previously arranged. This did not bode well for the Green-Fingered garden maintenance company.

When Adam came home that night, he was disappointed to find the grassy verges still uncut and enquired as to the commitment of the contractors. I explained the situation and he accepted it graciously. 'I guess these things happen,' he said.

The following day, yet again it was a bright fine morning. I was up early and decided to potter in the garden down by the garages. There were a few planters I wanted to pot up and I was planning to fashion a large hanging basket to go outside the front door – at my own expense, so as not to encounter the wrath of Francesco. I had noticed a large wrought-iron bracket next to the front door, and thought as a neighbourly gesture, I would hang up the basket for the residents to enjoy, adding a beautiful floral welcome to the visitors of Battlefields House.

It was nine fifteen and I was in the garage when I heard a van coming down the drive. It pulled up at the edge of the sloping car park. I looked up to see the garden maintenance contractor's van, complete with trailer. Positioned high on the back of the trailer and sitting very pretty was a bright shiny new state-of-the-art pristine mower. Adam would have been in awe of such a machine. I wished he was here to see it!

I watched from the security of my garage while two men alighted from the front seats of the van, dressed in white coveralls bearing the words GREEN FINGERS in dark green italic writing on the front. The older of the two came towards the house, while the younger of the two started uncoupling the trailer from the van. That completed, he climbed back up on to the mower and turned on the ignition, reversing down the trailer ramp, watching behind as he carefully negotiated the narrow gauge on which the mower wheels slowly turned.

Then it all happened in slow motion. As he reversed down the unhitched trailer, its end tipped up and the weight of the trailer now separated from the van set the van slowly in motion. With no one to stop the catastrophe about to unfold, the van, whose handbrake had not been fully applied, silently departed from its parked position, and moved off slowly in a downward direction towards the sloping bank. As it gained speed the youth looked up only to see the white van disappear over the edge of the bank and head for the woods. I stood rooted to the spot! It careered down the steep bank, crushing the undergrowth, snapping off branches and leaves as it trundled on out of control. The youth stood up on the mower to see the disaster in full swing, unable to do a thing about it.

The van now gained speed, careering through the woods, losing its wing mirrors on both sides as it bounced off the trees, and was now on a direct course for the greenhouse. It finally came to rest two meters inside the frame after completely demolishing the front of the building. Its glass shattered into fragments, the frame buckled and gave way, falling in several different directions, then the van groaned to a sudden halt, its catastrophic journey finally over. Terracotta pots, bamboo canes, shards of broken glass and wooden pieces of bench were strewn around the area bags of compost, garden tools, bulbs, tubers and unearthed seedlings were dispersed about the undergrowth. It looked like a market garden battlefield.

The youth stood rooted to the spot in shock and disbelief at what had just transpired. The noise of the calamity brought several residents out of their apartments, along with Francesco and the Green Fingers contractor, who rushed past me to see what all the commotion was about.

As they peered over the embankment at the wreckage the final piece of greenhouse framework gave up its precariously balanced position and crashed forward, breaking the only pane of glass that was not already shattered.

Francesco looked at the youth, who was traumatised by the event and was mumbling incomprehensibly to himself.

'What just bloody happened?' Francesco shouted at the youngster.

The older contractor went over and put his arm round the youngster, as he could see he was in shock over the incident, and told him not to worry and that it was not his fault, as he was the one who hadn't properly tightened the handbrake.

Francesco was livid! He paced back and forth like a bear with a sore head, threatening to sue for damages, ranting and raving at the lack of professionalism on the part of the contractor. Then he threw up his hands and said they would have to sort the problem out as he had an appointment in Bath and did not have the time or inclination to get the vehicle out of the mess they had caused. Not very helpful, I thought.

He stormed off in the direction of the house.

Jeremy and Jessica had now joined the group of inquisitive residents who had come out and were now congregating at the top of the embankment. A little line of bewildered, disbelieving people, they all stood surveying the sorry scene.

Jessica was distraught and had tears rolling down her face. I tried to console her, telling her that I would be there to help her sort everything out.

Jeremy took charge and suggested a towrope was needed to pull the van back up the embankment. Felix apparently had one that he kept in the cellar and ran off to get it. The decision was made to attach the towrope to the van and gradually pull it back up via the same route the vehicle had taken a few minutes earlier on its earth-shattering journey to the greenhouse.

This seemed a simple solution and in practice it should have worked but for one thing – the car that Jeremy was using to haul the van back up was not robust enough and after several attempts and much burning of tyre rubber and strain on the car engine, it was decided that maybe a tractor with more traction would be needed to complete the job in hand.

The numbers in the crowd now gathered were increasing, as friends of Felix had come down the drive in their car visiting for the afternoon and hastened over to see what the trouble was. Scratching their heads and rubbing their chins they gave their opinion of what should be done. The car they had arrived in was a Rover with a four-wheel drive and they assured Jeremy that it would be powerful enough to haul the van back up. One of them unhitched the towrope from the smaller car and attached it to the four-by-four as agreed by the organising party. He climbed in, starting the engine with a roar.

The Rover took the strain and gradually, as the rope stretched to its limit, the car inched forward, the wheels gripped the tarmac but alas after several minutes and much rallying and cheering by the crowd, the powerful vehicle was unable to budge the forsaken company van.

Francesco came out of the front door and, before driving off in his car for the afternoon, gave the contractors a malevolent stare, but never came over or gave helpful advice or his opinion on the situation.

Admitting defeat eventually, a phone call was made to the local farmer by Jeremy, asking for his assistance. It took over an hour before the farmer came trundling down the driveway in his large blue tractor and it was already getting dark. It dawned on me that the Green Fingers contractors had not had anything to eat or drink since they had arrived early that morning, so I offered them drinks and sandwiches.

They were delighted and demolished the ham offerings and two mugs of tea when I returned with a tray ten minutes later. By then the tractor had been coupled to the rope, which was in turn coupled to the vehicle down the embankment. The farmer released the handbrake and edged forward.

The rope tightened yet again, but we were all unsure if it would hold or indeed snap the towrope under so much strain. The tractor held its position for a minute then edged forward, pulling on the rope like the British Lions rugby team in a tug-o-war.

There was a cheer from the now-excited crowd, as the van moved slightly in the undergrowth, the framework of the greenhouse shuddered and groaned and a few pieces of glass fell to the ground. But the vehicle was moving, slowly at first, then the tractor pulled off and the wheels on the sorry van turned and moved slowly back up towards the top of the ridge. It retraced the tyre marks exactly as it reversed and gradually inch by inch it emerged from its position. The farmer was on course for a victory, and a round of applause and a whoop ensued from the interested onlookers. Eventually the rear wheels emerged at the top of the embankment and with a final engine rev from the victorious tractor the van was pulled over the ridge and bounced on all four tyres back into the car park, its wing mirror dangling loosely on one side like a lop-eared rabbit.

The crowd dispersed quickly as the entertainment was now over and stomachs were rumbling. The whole episode had taken nine hours and a lot of organisation and patience on behalf of all involved. The contractor opened the dented driver's door, which had a long scratch down the side, and tentatively climbed into the cab. He switched on the engine and immediately it started up. After putting it in reverse, he backed it into the car park and turned off the engine. Jeremy and the contractor spoke for several minutes and after shaking hands and their grateful thanks given to the farmer, the two Green-Fingered men hitched up the trailer, with the lawn mower now back on board and jumped in the mutilated van and drove off.

So yet again when Adam came home from work the grass had still not been mown.

A week later and returning from a nice afternoon out shopping with our son Ben, we saw Jessica come from the field beyond the house driving a bright blue sit-on-mower. She wore green dungarees, a matching cap and wellie boots, pulling a trolley and in matching attire was Jeremy. Apparently, Francesco had sacked the contractors, suing them for the cost of a replacement greenhouse and surrounding damaged woodland and had not organised for them to come back and finish the mowing contract. Therefore Jessica and Jeremy had taken it upon themselves to do the job.

Jessica waved excitedly as we neared the car park, then set off on the vehicle in a determined manner. Starting at one end of the lawn she continued across and down the slope until she reached the edge of the woods Turning very confidently she lined up the machine parallel to the first stripe in the lawn and continued in a very straight line until she had completed a second stripe. As we emptied the car boot of all the shopping, we could see a fourth stripe appear.

Jeremy was strimming the edge of the lawn and gave us a wave. I was pleased to see that the issue of the grass-cutting had been solved and J and J would have my vote when it came to the forthcoming management committee meeting next month. I would make sure of that.

CHAPTER 7

BLEEDING CANKER

The garden maintenance contract now taken over by number 4 had made a big improvement to the landscaping round the house. The lawns were tidy and beautifully striped, the clippings were gathered and disposed of in the woods and the edges of the driveway were not irregular as they had been previously and even the banks were neat and trim. Adam commented on what a good job was being done by our new neighbours.

The previous contractors had written an apology to the Battlefields Management Committee members offering to replace the glasshouse and pay for any damage caused. Francesco had written in reply saying that would be acceptable but had cancelled the contract with them, having had no conversation whatsoever with the other members of the committee.

Sitting up in my ivory tower, as Ben called it, I could see quite a lot of what went on unobserved by most people. It was nice to sit there enjoying the wonderful views early in the morning drinking a hot coffee in my dressing gown and unkempt hair without worrying about being seen by the neighbours.

On one occasion a few weeks later while sitting there, I

noticed Felix and Jeremy wandering along together, stopping at every chestnut tree that lined the driveway from the top to the bottom. They were beautiful chestnut trees, hundreds of years old. The two men stopped at the last tree at the end of the route and stood for several minutes staring up into the branches, pointing and gesturing at the crown of the tree.

I wondered what they were discussing as it looked like they were concerned about something. Then I remembered at the previous management meeting Jeremy had brought up a concern over mildew and leaf drop in some of the chestnut trees. A few days later, a note was pushed under the door, a regular occurrence now Adam had become chairman, and the problem became clear.

There was great concern over the largest chestnut tree losing its leaves early in the year, as they had discussed previously. The leaves were turning brown and wilting and there was a yellow ring of mildew round the root area of two trees. Jeremy and Felix were requesting a meeting to discuss the problem and to come up with a solution as to what should be done, if anything.

Hoping to avoid yet another meeting, Adam phoned number four and after a long in-depth conversation, volunteered to give his friend Charlie a ring to see if he would come out and run his expert eye over the problem. Adam apologised for not following up his promise of calling Charlie earlier and would phone him immediately. As previously mentioned, his friend was Charlie Samplar, an old acquaintance.

He was a useful guy to know, especially as he was a qualified tree surgeon and landscape expert. He ran a one-man operation and had been running a successful business for twenty years.

Charlie was a middle-aged man who had kept himself in good shape over the years. His physical work of tree surgery was strenuous, hauling himself up amongst the tree tops, working with chainsaws, and with wicket-keeping as his hobby, he was in good health. He had a mop of yellow hair that was never tidy and a little longer than it needed to be.

Charlie was a little shy around groups of people and seemed a quiet, thoughtful human being. He had never married to our knowledge and never brought anyone to watch him play cricket. He seemed a bit of a loner but he and Adam had become firm friends, so it was no surprise when Charlie agreed to come out to see us. He would visit the following week and give us his opinion on the problem.

The meeting was to be held on a Saturday at ten o'clock and Adam, Felix and Jeremy waited for Charlie down by the affected trees. Charlie was very punctual, as we knew him to be, and rolled up in his van at precisely 10 a.m. I could see them from our upstairs window, deep in discussion as they walked up the avenue of trees, stopping and talking as they went. Charlie walked round several chestnuts, pulling at bits of bark and turning over lumps of earth from around the roots with a small trowel. It was not looking good!

After at least an hour I saw Charlie shake hands and was waved off the premises as he turned up the drive in his white van.

Adam came in and sat down. 'That was interesting,' he said. 'Charlie was very knowledgeable about the subject; he acknowledged we have a serious problem with most of the chestnuts. He said the horse chestnut tree can often succumb to a disease known as "bleeding canker", caused by a fungus called

Guighardia Aesculi. He knows his stuff. Apparently, the disease produces reddish or dull brown patches that are concentrated on the tips of the infected leaves, which means they die and fall off the tree early.'

I asked if there was anything that could be done, but Adam shook his head and said the only remedy was to chop the trees down. They would eventually rot anyway and might in years to come prove dangerous if there were winter storms.

A little drastic I thought!

He would report his findings to the management committee next month and Charlie's recommendations and take it from there.

A few weeks later we had storm warnings in our area, a depression was forecast on the local weather station, and it looked like the weekend was going to be blustery and very wet.

We planned to have our eldest son, Thomas, up for lunch on the Sunday. Thomas lived approximately twenty miles away and worked full-time as a personal trainer. He was busy during the day and some evenings so it was always a high point when he could come for a Sunday lunch with us.

His brother Ben was looking forward to catching up and beating him at a game of FIFA World Cup on his new PlayStation. We planned a roast lamb lunch, his favourite, with roast potatoes, carrots, cauliflower, roast parsnip and mint jelly, which he always insisted upon, followed by home-made apple pie and cream.

Adam volunteered to peel the potatoes, while Ben laid the table for lunch. He popped a few bottles of beer in the fridge, and a bottle of red wine was put on the table alongside napkins and the best glasses from the cupboard. It was going to be a nice family day together.

Or so I thought!

Eleven thirty came and the lunch was well under way, but the wind outside was picking up – we could see from the kitchen window the force of the gale as it whipped the tops of the trees into a frenzy. Dark clouds were forming and it had started to rain, lightly at first then really heavily.

I looked out of the lounge window, wondering if Thomas was already on his way, as he was expected about 12 p.m. for lunch. He should be here soon and would have to make a run for cover from the car park.

With that thought, his silver Audi came down the drive and parked up in the crowded car park. It seemed there were many visitors to Battlefields today. He climbed out and, with a jacket over his head, ran to the front door. I heard the bell ring and quickly pressed the front door release button so he could enter the hallway downstairs.

I opened the front door to the apartment as he came bounding up the stairs two at a time and greeted me with a big hug and a kiss – it was so good to see him! Even though he kept in touch by phone, texting every other day, it did not make up for that big hug. Just seeing him was a joy. Ben was delighted to see him too and gave him a brotherly hug. Adam was the next in line, slapping Thomas on the back and commenting on his new haircut. Soon enough the banter started between them all. It was great to see them together, enjoying each other's company.

As boys they had grown up very close to each other, being

only three years apart. Thomas had a great sense of humour and saw the funny side of things – his outlook on life was always positive and uplifting. His love for his younger brother was obvious and the feeling was mutual. Ben had always looked up to his older sibling and admired him for his protective qualities and the sense of fun and the hilarious banter that ricocheted between them making us all laugh. Ben was a little more serious in his outlook – he had a keen sense of justice and fairness and was always a calming influence in a crisis. His caring qualities and the desire to help others were a credit to him and we could see why he aspired to eventually join the police force. If he could achieve his degree in sociology and criminology while at Bristol University, he stood a good chance of becoming a first-class officer in the constabulary.

But for now, they were just two brothers looking forward to a roast lunch cooked by their slightly dotty mother and potato-peeling, fun-loving father.

As the lunch was underway and the potatoes were roasting in the oven, we had time for a drink and a catch-up on all their news while we sat round the kitchen table. We told them of the progress we were making and of all the plans we had to improve not only our apartment but of our aspirations here at Battlefields House.

Ben was still a little unsure of his feelings about living in such a strange place, but for now he had a roof over his head, his meals were cooked for him, his dirty socks were picked up after he forgot to put them in the linen bin, and he could come and go as he pleased. He was very lucky and he knew and appreciated that fact. He was saving all his money that he earned working part-time and after graduating from university, he was intending to buy a small place of his own.

Lunch was served in the dining room as the wind continued to blow gale-force outside. The rain beat down and thunder was heard in the distance. I reminded Ben as I had done when he was frightened as a boy, how you counted the seconds between the thunder and the lightning and then you could calculate how far from the worst of the storm you were. We could see lightning streaking across the sky in the distance. It forked across, leaving jagged zigzags of intense white light against the ever-darkening sky. It looked quite menacing.

Just as we finished our lunch and were looking forward to apple pie and cream, the lights went out!

'Oh, bugger,' said Adam. 'Do we have any candles?'

I left the table and in the dim light rummaged around in the drawer of the cupboard, pulling out a box of matches. After striking a match I could make out the cupboard door and felt inside for a box of taper candles and a holder I had bought for Christmas.

The tapers were lit and placed in the middle of the table.

'This is romantic,' Adam said.

The lightning was cracking overhead by now and occasionally the room lit up with the intensity of the lightning strikes. I was concerned that being so high up on a hill we might get a direct hit, but Adam assured me there were lightning conductors round the turrets and there was no possibility of such a thing happening!

I found a few more candles and dotted them around the room, giving the place an eerie, rather than romantic feel.

'It is like a haunted house in a horror movie,' Thomas joked. 'I can see why Ben's not so happy living here – did you see the eyes move on your twin lookalike painting, Ben?' he teased.

Adam went to look out of the window as the rain lashed across the blackened pane. The rain was coming down heavily and it was so dark without the electricity.

Thomas said, 'It looks like the world has come to an end and we are the only people left.' I told him not to be so melodramatic and that he would scare the pants off Ben if he kept on with his not-so-funny jokes.

I felt my way to the kitchen and found a torch in the drawer, while Adam brought out the empty plates and stacked them in the dishwasher. Picking up the warm apple pie, I carried it into the lounge and set it on the table. Adam came in with the cream and we set about cutting and serving the delicious pie, trying to make light of the situation.

Just as Thomas was about to take his first bite of the piecrust there was a streak of lightning that lit up the room, followed by an almighty crash outside the window.

'Did you see that?' shrieked Ben. 'It was fork lightning!'

'More like a bolt of lightning!' shouted Thomas. 'Perhaps it struck the building.'

We left the apple pie except for Ben, who continued eating his from the bowl as we rushed over to the window and looked out.

Sure enough, a bolt of lightning had struck one of the chestnut trees that lined the driveway. The tree was actually on fire and leaning at an odd angle towards the building. It looked precarious and was being battered by the high winds. Gradually the flames were diminishing due to the heavy rain, but the tree was being tossed back and forth like a loose tooth on a sinewy thread. As we stood looking out of the window, the tree lurched forward once more towards the building, then it was torn away again in the opposite direction.

'It's going to come down,' said Adam, 'but in which direction is it going to fall?'

His question was shortly answered as the tree lunged once more towards the house, but then seemed to be pulled away again by an invisible hand, back away from the house. It gave an almighty crack as it fell to the ground like a wounded animal after being shot in the heart.

The smouldering trunk had missed the house by sheer luck, or was it phantom intervention? But it had inconveniently fallen right across the driveway, blocking the only route from the house to the main road.

'Well, that's you stuck for the night,' said Adam. 'Looks like you won't be going anywhere soon,' he said to Thomas.

Thomas had just resigned himself to a night spent in Ben's room on the floor or a sleeping bag on the settee when there was a ring on the intercom.

It was Francesco – he wanted Adam to come down to the hall, where he was forming a working party to remove the tree trunk from the drive. Adam really could not believe what he was hearing!

'Can it wait until the morning?' I heard Adam saying into the intercom connection. *Obviously not!* was the indignant reply from the other end of the intercom.

Adam pulled his coat on and put on his walking boots, not too happy about going out into the storm. He told us all to wait and see what was being proposed by the rest of the residents before we could decide what should be done. We waited for him to return and continued clearing away the dishes, realising that due to the power cut we would have to wash up by hand.

Fifteen minutes passed before Adam came back up with the news that we were all needed down in the hall where Francesco would be organising us into groups. We were to bring saws, tree loppers and torches if we owned any and dress for bad weather.

Thomas said that was an understatement, and that the weather was too dangerous for people to go out into. We all agreed but Adam stated that he had not been able to talk Francesco out of waiting until the storm abated, and we would have to go and help remove the huge trunk from the driveway.

I went to the basement to find wellington boots and wet gear that we only used on rare occasions. Today was one of those rare occasions.

When we were finally kitted out, we all met up in the hallway where Michael, Francesco, Felix and Jeremy were already discussing tactics on how we should go about removing the obstructing article. Jeremy, being a man of machinery, had a petrol-driven chainsaw in his lock-up down in the field they rented and hastened to get it. As he opened the front door, it swung back, buffeted by the gusty wind, and a deluge of rain swept into the hallway. He put his hood up and pulled the heavy door behind him, disappearing out into the darkness with only a little torch beam to light his way.

A selection of tools lay scattered around the floor: several handsaws, a large pair of tree loppers and a tarpaulin sheet, also a long length of rope. What this was for was beyond my comprehension, but I was ready to help in any way I could. *Many hands make light work* my father always told me. I did notice there were no other female residents willing to join in the task. Probably all watching from the comfort of a window while the men of Battlefields literally battled the elements.

After Jeremy returned with the angry-looking chainsaw, bedraggled and quite anxious, we followed Francesco out into the darkness. The wind was very strong and tore at our clothing as we made our way towards the fallen tree. It was making it difficult to walk and still the rain came down in torrents. We were glad to have wet gear on as we would have been soaked to the skin otherwise.

Jeremy, now in charge and without any hesitation, started up the power tool. It roared into life and we all stood back as he attacked the branches, lopping off huge pieces as he methodically worked his way round the log. He was quite accomplished in handling such a large piece of equipment and soon three or four yards along the trunk had been cleared.

Having stripped the area lying across the driveway, he then proceeded to cut diagonal chunks out of the main tree. It became apparent that he was only going to remove the large middle section of the trunk, thus leaving enough room to drive a car through for the residents who needed to get to work the following day. Francesco had agreed that the main trunk of the tree could be left until the weather improved, then we would need to return and finish the job.

As Jeremy continued his attack on the branches, we started clearing all the debris. The tarpaulin was used to carry the branches and discarded wood from the tree. We piled it all up and hauled it down to the woods.

Jeremy handed over to Felix after he complained that his shoulders were beginning to ache. The tree was wet and difficult to cut but after a couple of hours we were making good progress. The tree was now sub-divided into smaller sections and each section was just about manageable. The rope was tied securely round the first chunk, and we pulled to remove it from the main tree. This worked well – the log was rolled away and stacked nearby.

We continued to work in this way while the wind blew like an Atlantic storm, nearly knocking us off our feet. Thomas and Ben, as usual in any dire situation, joked and laughed their way through the whole episode, competing to see who could offload the most branches on to the trolley that Jeremy had found. It took us hours to finally clear enough room for the driveway to be free of the tree and for us to return to our apartments to dry off. It was a job well done, we had all contributed to the task and Francesco thanked everyone for their concerted effort.

Adam commented afterwards that great things could be achieved if everyone got involved. I hoped that this would continue, as many things required attention around the house, and it needed a willingness and camaraderie to achieve this from everyone that lived here.

The following day, the wind had subsided, and the rain had ceased to fall in torrents. Outside, the trees were now still after the battering they had received the previous night and stood dripping and lank. The fallen chestnut lay stricken across the driveway minus the large chunk that had been removed.

Thomas had risen early and after a quick breakfast was heading out of the apartment and off to work, saying his goodbyes in a hurry as he picked up a piece of Ben's freshly buttered toast. Waving it under his brother's nose, he laughed and said thanks. Ben instantly came back with a quick-witted joke and proceeded to pop another piece of bread into the toaster. The door closed behind Thomas after a hug and a peck on the cheek and I wandered into the lounge to watch from the turret window as he drove up the drive, slowing down as he manoeuvred his pride and joy through the segmented trunk of the fallen tree. He disappeared round the curve in the lane.

The rest of the day was going to be spent in taking down all the old, discoloured curtain tracks that had been left behind after Walter had vacated the apartment. Ben was due to attend a lecture that afternoon so I requested that he might help me for an hour or so. The ceiling was very high in the apartment, and I was going to need a long ladder to reach the top of the coving where the offending articles were screwed securely to the wall. There was such a ladder in the basement, which although belonging to the house we were permitted to use for any occasion necessary.

As Ben had not yet ventured into the bowels of the Battlefields mansion, I was interested in his thoughts on that part of the building. We descended the stone steps into the basement in silence. As I grappled for the light switch, I noticed there was a light coming from under one of the cellar doors just along from ours. I commented to Ben about it, thinking it of no real consequence, but as we spoke the light instantly went out. We stopped in our tracks. I eventually found the light switch and flicked it on, bringing a dim luminescence to the underground vault. I was glad Ben was with me. Not to be alarmed by the sudden absence of the light behind the door, I called out, 'It's only me!' I waited for a reply, but none came. Ben, being a little more assertive and impatient to get to the bottom of the mystery, turned the handle of the closed door expecting it to open and reveal whoever was inside. The door appeared locked and after several attempts to open it, he looked at me and shrugged.

'Must be locked from the inside,' he whispered. Inquisitive in nature Ben bent down and tried to look through the keyhole.

'Ben,' I whispered, trying not to giggle, 'stop it! You are too suspicious – I'm sure there is a reasonable explanation for the light going out.'

But Ben was having none of it. He started sniffing at the keyhole.

'What are you doing?' I whispered.

'Ascertaining if there is drug misuse.'

I pulled him away from the door and ushered him to the bottom of the steps. 'Don't be ridiculous, this is a respectable place. You don't really expect me to believe that one of our neighbours is growing cannabis in the basement, do you?' I asked with a worried frown on my face.

'Mum, you would be surprised what respectable people get up to. Nothing would surprise me out here – it is a perfect hideaway. Which of your neighbours do you imagine would be brazen enough to be growing cannabis plants behind a locked door down here away from prying eyes?' he quizzed.

'Well, does it smell like cannabis?' I questioned as he sniffed again at the keyhole

He admitted that he could not smell anything unusual except the dank, musty aroma that was usually found in such a place.

I ruffled his hair and told him he had too much imagination and would make a great detective one of these days. Especially if he actually did some written work on the subject towards his university degree.

We eventually located the extra-lengthy ladder and managed to carry it between us back up to the apartment where we placed it against the wall in readiness for my afternoon exertions.

On many occasions and to quell his inquisitive mind Ben often brought the subject up and asked on a regular basis if I had smelt anything suspicious in the basement. We never did find out who was behind the locked basement door or what their secretive intentions were, but I did have a crafty sniff at the keyhole whenever I ventured down into the cellar on the odd occasion, just to satisfy my curiosity.

CHAPTER 8

THE GREENHOUSE

We had been quite pleased how things were going during the first few months at the house. Every month we were due to hold a management committee meeting, but this month it had been cancelled due to Francesco being away in Italy visiting relatives. He had been gone three weeks and was due back the day after tomorrow, therefore it had been decided to postpone the set date long enough for him to return and attend the meeting. He was required to give a treasurer's report every month and it was necessary for him to be present.

Adam had sent round an invitation to all residents inviting them round for a drink and nibbles. This was to take place in our apartment. Even though the state of repair of the lounge and hallway was not suitable to entertain people, we felt we had no real choice in the matter, as the chairperson had always hosted the meeting in the past and we were expected by Francesco to uphold this tradition.

On the day of the meeting, I decided to bake some cupcakes, so these could be served with tea or coffee to our guests later that evening. This completed and sitting in the turret window drinking my coffee, I saw a lorry head down the drive. On the back of the trailer were square panels of aluminium; there were also stacked panes of glass bound up in bubble wrap.

It must be the new greenhouse, I thought to myself. The Green-Fingered contractor had come through with his promise of a replacement greenhouse and they were obviously here to erect it, I watched as the new frame was unloaded and taken by the two men round the back of the garage, where they disappeared from sight. It was a shame about what had happened but at least we were going to have a replacement potting frame and, in all honesty a newer version was really needed as the previous greenhouse had been at least fifty years old and had seen better days. So maybe it had been a blessing in disguise after all.

I ventured out later in the day to see how things were progressing, and I was surprised how well the two guys were getting on. The new aluminium frame was already standing on the old concrete base, but it seemed much bigger than the old wooden greenhouse that had encountered the van. In fact, they had extended the new build at least three feet longer than it had been before. This was going to be an impressive building, and I was sure Jessica would be delighted when she saw it.

It was later in the day when I popped down again, this time taking two mugs of tea for the workers. They were very pleased to stop for a quick break before returning to finish off the build. They were keen to get the glasshouse finished to avoid running into Francesco, as they stated they had managed to avoid him and did not wish to run into him ever again. I thanked them for their hard work and apologised for the lack of understanding shown by Francesco in the past. They finally finished the job the next day just in time before Francesco returned from his vacation.

The cupcakes were iced that afternoon with grated lime and mascarpone cheese and as Adam came home from work, he commented on how delicious they looked, pinching one before I could tap him on the knuckles with my wooden spoon.

'They're delicious,' he said as he munched his way through the sponge cake. I told him they were for the evening's committee meeting, and he grinned saying that Francesco really didn't deserve such a luxury and that he hoped he was in a lighter mood now he had returned from his holiday and the greenhouse had been replaced.

I commented on the excellent job done on the replacement and told Adam I had spoken to the contractors and apologised for the rudeness of Francesco. He agreed that there was no need for Francesco's bad manners but hoped that now number four had taken over the contract he himself was more likely to get a chance to reach his objective in securing a free ride on the mower.

I told him I was not so sure as Jessica and Jeremy were very proud of their new equipment and might not be so willing to let it out of their sight and allow a rookie grass cutter loose on their beautifully manicured lawn. He laughed as he went out of the kitchen and into the bedroom to change for the meeting.

CHAPTER 9

AXMINSTER RED

Francesco was in such good spirits when he came into our apartment that evening as his holiday had been enjoyed and had obviously been a remedy for his bad disposition. The Italian sun had browned his furrowed brow a few shades darker, and he looked a little more relaxed than I had seen him a month earlier.

After all the residents who were attending the meeting had found a chair or seat to sit on, the minutes were read out by Adam as newly appointed chairman and discussions started about the gardening contract, now taken over temporarily by J and J.

After many reservations raised by Francesco, backed up with an equal passion by Lena, Adam put the proposal to a vote. My hand was the first to go up in favour of the new contract going to number four, with Felix representing his apartment also voting to back the venture. Daniel and the newly introduced Felicity, his wife, cast their vote in favour and Adam read an abstention from Cordelia Whipsnake at number two. She was absent from the meeting and had sent her apologies but had confessed in a brief note on Battlefields headed notepaper slipped under our door, she felt, as she had only moved into Battlefields in the spring, she felt she really didn't know which way to vote and would leave the decision to better-informed residents.

Lena had the permission of the absent couple from number five to vote any way she saw fit and so cast their vote as a nay rather than a yea. Nevertheless the motion was passed and Jessica and Jeremy were delighted to have received the majority of the residents votes and secure the garden contract.

The thoughts on the summer fundraising event were not so enthusiastic as they had been at the last meeting. It was felt that the summer was turning into autumn and the weather was changing. Francesco thought we had left it too late to organise.

I thought he might be right this time and suggested we plan it for the summer of next year instead. This was agreed and Adam pencilled it into his notes to raise the subject again in the spring of the following year. This would give us all time to concentrate our ideas and make it a successful event in the future.

One item on the agenda for discussion for the second time was the chestnut trees and the professional advice given freely by Adam's friend Charlie Samplar. After reiterating Charlie's thoughts, Adam was surprised when Francesco suddenly stood up, why he stood up we did not know – and said he was definitely against taking any of the diseased trees down. Adam pointed out that they could prove a possible danger in the future, especially if we had many more storms like the one, we'd had recently.

Felicity was concerned and stated that cutting any tree down was a no-no and she looked at her husband for support. Felicity loved the trees and could not imagine the chestnut-lined driveway without them. She had a point – even I was loathe to see them felled.

Helen and Michael voted not to remove them at present and wanted to wait and see what condition they were in before next winter.

As Lena had the vote for number five and again Cordelia had abstained from adding her vote one way or the other – the motion was voted down. The trees would remain standing upright for the foreseeable future. Unless the forces of nature decided otherwise. Motion denied.

The next item raised by Adam was the carpet replacement on the stairway and he passed the baton to me. This was where I stepped in to update the residents on my progress on the carpet project, and from a box I pulled out several carpet samples, a wide range of colour swatches and a costing per square metre depending on the quality of the carpet chosen.

This was passed round, and a few comments were spoken in favour of one sample. The best quality proved to be the Axminster carpet, the wool content had proved an important factor in the decision to go top end, even though there were a few disenchanted mutterings coming from Francesco's corner on cost.

Felix mentioned that you got what you paid for where carpet was concerned, and he was voting for the Axminster 100% wool. It was passed round once again, and the decision was voted on positively that we should invest in the better end of the range as quality would endure the ravages of time.

The next decision was a little more complicated and the choice of colour was proving a sticking point. The discussion carried on for an hour, the samples were plain in nature; I had not included any patterned samples since the present covering was plain, so I had assumed it would be replaced with a plain not patterned style. This had been a mistake on my part, but Adam was backing me up on this point and so were Jessica and Jeremy. Even though they would probably hardly ever set foot on the carpet themselves they agreed plain would be best for the stairwell.

The person whom I least expected to take part so fervently in the deliberations was Helen. She had been indifferent previously when the carpet replacement had been mentioned, and she had hoped to see some patterned samples and was disappointed that I had not included any.

Nobody else backed her objection or supported her in her preference of pattern, so she withdrew her objections and reluctantly agreed to go with the plain option. She fidgeted in her chair thereafter and seemed to lose interest in the discussions.

Next was the colour choice. I had picked out several colours that I thought would enhance the stairway: a deep French Mustard that tied in with the painted walls in the hall downstairs; a Royal Red that I thought would look very regal. I had seen the colour used in Buckingham Palace in the King's Gallery and thought if it was good enough for His Royal Highness then it was good enough for Battlefields House. The final colour was Buttermilk Cream.

The three apartments it affected the most from a colour perspective were numbers one, two and us at number three. The carpet meandered from the high-ceilinged hallway to the top of the building, passing our apartment before it rolled on up to the landing past Cordelia's front door at number two, finally ending at Michael and Helen's apartment number one. Therefore, it was decided by the members that these apartment occupiers should agree on the colour choice between themselves.

I favoured the Royal Red swatch along with Adam, and Helen and Michael went for the French Mustard, so it was agreed that Cordelia would be consulted and out of the two chosen hues, her choice would make the final decision. I agreed to leave the two preferred samples in the hallway on the large sideboard in an envelope for Cordelia to peruse at her leisure and whichever one she chose I would arrange for the carpet contractors to come out and give the members a quote for the whole job.

The following weekend when Cordelia was spotted entering the hallway by Lena, she was approached for her decision and stated that she preferred the Royal Red. Decision made!

On contacting the carpet contractors the following week, the first question they asked was whether we wanted the old carpet removed and disposed of, as this would require extra payment for removal and a skip hire for a few days.

I needed a quick decision on this outcome as I had left the conversation with the carpet company up in the air. We hoped to get the new carpet laid this side of Christmas and time was ticking.

After spotting Francesco entering the hallway downstairs the following afternoon, on his way in from the garden, I rushed down the cantilever stairway and accosted him by the front door, explaining the need to make an instant decision on the carpet removal. He listened intently as I put my case, nodding then frowning, which was disconcerting as he looked very menacing when his eyebrows furrowed and his lower lip was bitten, like a hairy spider eyeing up a struggling bluebottle caught in its web.

I stuck to my point, as Adam had always said, *say whatever it is with certainty and conviction and keep to the point.* All this was going through my head as I was talking to Francesco, but I found myself gradually losing my confidence under his gaze and I could see he was wavering on his decision. I was so desperate to achieve a positive outcome having got this far that from somewhere out of the blue and without thinking, I suddenly found myself volunteering to repaint the black wrought-iron balustrade and white-gloss the stone steps from top to bottom free of charge to save on the financial outlay. All this I would do before the new carpet was laid, I added just as suddenly.

Adam's inspiring words had abandoned me, and my voice became a mere whisper. Had I given away too much in my effort to get Francesco onside?

After much deliberation and not having any other money-saving schemes that he could come up with, his face lit up! He could suddenly now see the financial gain in having the stairway freshened up at no extra cost, except to myself, and he heartily agreed to allow the hiring of a skip for a few days while the experts removed the old sun-faded covering and disposed of it.

Well, Adam's face was not smiling when I told him of my offer. He really thought I had fallen into the age-old trap of giving away far too much at the negotiating table and wished he had been there to give me some support. I understood his concerns but at least now we could organise the removal of the offending covering and get things sorted out by Christmas.

Unfortunately, I had given myself and Adam a week's work, first removing the old carpet, then rubbing down and repainting the steps and black metal balustrade prior to the fitting of the new carpet.

We had arranged for the stair covering to be delivered in two weeks allowing the carpet fitters to measure up and do whatever was necessary prior to that date, so everything had to be finished and dry before the Friday. The cantilever stairs were of an age that they had not been made industrially but cut individually from local stone. Some were specifically cut to fit the interior wall that curved and spiralled upwards, so it proved to be a labour-intensive job when the fitters finally came to lay the Axminister. By then the wrought ironwork was freshly painted glossy black, and the stonework was looking smooth and lustrous. It took them two days to lay the beautiful royal red river of carpet that flowed from top to bottom of the house; it looked like a scarlet ribbon as it curved its way down. It was stunning!

At the next management committee meeting it was noted in the minutes that everyone had approved the project and that it was a fantastic improvement to the stairway. Helen sent her apologies ahead of the meeting as she was unable to attend because she had a nail appointment!

CHAPTER 10

THE ROOFING PROJECT

At the last committee meeting Adam had raised the felt-roofing replacement item again. This covered the area above our kitchen and was due to take place before winter came. It had been given the go-ahead by the committee members and Jeremy had remarked at the time that it had been due to be replaced last year, but with Walter still in charge and unwilling to make the commitment or financial go-ahead, and Francesco complaining about the financial cost, nothing had been done.

Jeremy was concerned not for himself but for us. He had inspected our area of the roof last time he was up there checking for maintenance problems and stone renovations that might need attention and had seen a few potential bird-nesting sites that had disrupted the felt near the bottom slate tiles.

It was agreed that a roofer would be employed to remove existing roof tiles and re-felt the whole area above our kitchen. We were delighted that this was going ahead as it had been a concern to Adam when we purchased number three.

As Jeremy was maintenance officer for Battlefields, which was on a volunteer basis, he kept an eye on potential hazards, pre-empting any disastrous situations waiting to happen and warning us all any impending maintenance issues that needed addressing.

Any funding for house projects would be taken out of the financial pot, which never seemed very full. The felt covering and removal and subsequent replacement would cost £10,000 so it was a large sum of money involved in the project. Nevertheless, it had been agreed and Jeremy would oversee the project.

It was left for us to talk to Jeremy and make arrangements for the project to start as soon as possible before winter got underway.

Jeremy was happy and somewhat relieved to contact the roofing company had come out previously to give estimates and view the problem, so things started to happen quite quickly. We were informed the project would start the following month and would take approximately two weeks from start to finish. Luckily the weather was good and, as promised, the scaffolding was erected two weeks later.

In the middle of this, I had been involved with the new kitchen design and restructuring, the old units had been removed and the new cupboards and equipment were being fitted. The floor covering had been taken up and disposed of, the ceiling plaster had been skimmed over and a beautiful simple cornice with ornate ceiling rose had been fitted with the drop chandelier I had chosen a few months earlier. It was all starting to come together.

The roofing contractors were very committed and, after a few days, were well into the project. I saw them from the kitchen window as they removed large pieces of dirty black felt and pushed it down the disposal tube that fed a large skip placed outside on the lawn. It soon filled up and as they passed the window, they often gave me a wave.

One morning while sitting in the kitchen drinking coffee, admiring the fine new units that had been fitted the previous day, I noticed a drip appear from the cornice on the ceiling and run down the freshly painted wall opposite me. I stared at it in disbelief as it dribbled in a long straight line and eventually stopped on the kitchen unit.

Moving from my chair I saw to my horror another drip follow the same path, joining the first drip as it mingled in a tiny pool on the worktop. I leaned over and grabbed the kitchen towel from the rail and dabbed up the pool of water. It soaked up the offending wet patch quickly, only for me to watch in horror as another dribble took its place. Very concerned, I immediately climbed up on to the chair to get a closer look, trying to see where this water was coming from exactly, but failed to see anything remotely unusual. It seemed to come out from behind the cornice – the newly painted, freshly plastered cornice!

The dribble continued and seemed to increase in volume, much to my distress. I shouted to Ben who was in his room studying. I was becoming increasingly upset by what was happening and my voice rose to a high-pitched wail as he came through the kitchen door to find me almost in tears, holding a handful of paper towels up over the space where the water seeped in.

'What's happened?' he said as he gazed up at me in my dressing gown and slippers standing on the sink unit holding untold pieces of wet and dripping paper towel to the ceiling.

I cried out, 'Get some towels – we have a leak coming through the ceiling!' He bolted off to the airing cupboard and returned a minute later carrying a towel. He passed it up to me and asked again what was happening.

'I don't know, but we've got to stop the water coming in; get more towels quickly!' I shouted, as he raced off again down the hall. Tears suddenly streamed down my face, built up from the feeling of the helpless situation I found myself in. I tried to stem the flow of liquid coming from the ceiling, but the towels got wetter and wetter.

Ben rushed over to the window and opened it wide. He shouted out to the roofing contractor, who rushed down the ladder and peered in the kitchen window.

'What the hell?' he muttered as he stuck his head in through the opening. 'I'll go and see what's happening up on the roof,' he said alarmed as he rushed back up the ladder.

Nothing happened for at least ten minutes. Ben brought in sheets from the airing cupboard to help stem the leak. We thought we might be able to limit the damage if we could prevent any water seeping under the units on to the floor.

Eventually, just as my arms were starting to go numb from supporting the wet sheets the contractor's face appeared at the window again. 'I've located the problem,' he said. 'The water should stop coming in any moment; hold on there just a bit longer'

I eased the towels away from the wall and held my breath as we watched to see if it had ceased. We watched as the dribble turned into a drip, then one final drip until it stopped completely.

'Has it stopped?' the contractor asked. It had, so I dropped the soggy pillow into the sink and climbed warily down with Ben's help. 'There was a space between the felting and the guttering where rainwater had collected from the last rain we had,' the builder said apologetically 'Jim must have dislodged the covering and the large pool of water ran down the beam, meandering its way to the lowest point of entry, without him realising it.'

He climbed in through the window to assess the damage. It appeared to him it was not as bad as first appeared and the insurance would cover any repainting or replastering that was necessary. 'Keep the radiator on in the kitchen and it will soon dry out,' was his suggestion.

It turned out he was correct in his advice and after the wall was repainted and a touch of emulsion on the plaster coving the following week it was as good as new. Disaster averted! Just.

CHAPTER 11

CHRISTMAS PUNCH AND PINE NEEDLES

Christmas was creeping up on us and it was a pleasant surprise one afternoon to receive a folded note under the door, inviting us down to the hall for a seasonal gathering. Lena and Francesco were offering a Christmas get-together on Saturday 23 December, an annual event that they had hosted for several years.

It had become a Battlefields tradition for all residents to congregate on the Saturday before Christmas at six o'clock for a glass of Christmas punch and a small spread laid on by Lena. We were welcome to bring a small selection of nibbles to share but primarily the spread would be provided by number seven.

We were very excited by this and sent our thanks via a notelet back to Lena and Francesco saying that we would be delighted to attend, and there would be three of us as Ben was enthusiastic to attend the Christmas event too.

Prior to this we had been informed by Felix that another Christmas tradition at Battlefields was the erection of a Christmas tree in the hallway. If Adam was available, he being the chairman, could choose the tree from the wooded area behind the house and Felix and Jeremy would fell it and help bring it into the hall where a large stand would be waiting for it to stand in. Between them all they would erect the tree in the corner of the great room for everyone to decorate the following weekend.

Adam was really pleased to be asked and, getting into the Christmas spirit, suggested we might have a real Christmas tree in our apartment. It was a splendid idea and two weeks before the twenty-fifth, we set off to buy our very own authentic traditional tree. We had always had an artificial tree in the past, but Adam's enthusiasm was catching, and he and Ben were keen to start a new tradition of a having a real pine Christmas tree. So, we set off, roof-rack on the top of the car, to purchase the said tree.

We went to the local Christmas tree farm shop where they had a huge selection, ranging from little tabletop rooted specimens to trees that were thirty feet tall.

We walked around the farmyard looking at all the different heights and varieties not knowing which one to choose. Suddenly from behind a large green spruce a head popped out – it was the farmer who had helped us out when the garden contractors van had careered down the embankment. He turned out to be the owner of the Christmas tree yard, and it was his farm we were visiting. His name was Edwin, and he was a jolly fellow. After recalling the unfortunate event back in the summer and receiving our thanks once again for stepping in to help with the van, he invited us into his kitchen behind the yard to warm up by the fire. He offered us hot chocolate that was bubbling on the range. His two sons were helping him out now, selling and bagging up the trees, but they were both really busy with family issues and could only lend their time on an ad-hoc basis. He was struggling to keep up with the demand and was not sure how he was going to cope over the next few weekends when his sons were not there to help him.

An idea struck me out of the blue. Ben was not doing anything for the next few weekends; he was home from university now he had broken up and he was at a loose end. I volunteered his services straight away. 'You could help out, couldn't you, Ben?' I asked. He shot me a look like I had suggested he fly to the moon, but stammered a 'Well . . . I suppose I could.'

He frowned at me behind farmer Edwin's back, obviously not too keen. He liked his warm home comforts and standing in the farmyard selling Christmas trees was not his idea of fun, even for a fortnight. Nevertheless, he agreed to come the following Saturday and Sunday to help.

One good turn deserves another, as my father had often said to me, and that thought I passed down the McKenzie heritage line on many occasions. We left Edwin saying we would return for the McKenzie Christmas tree when he was less busy.

It turned out that Edwin paid Ben handsomely for the following two weekends and he also picked up almost the same again in tips from grateful customers when he hoisted the netted trees into their open boots or tied the trees on to their roof-racks. He even admitted he had offered to help Edwin the following December to bag up the Christmas trees, if he needed a strong pair of hands.

On his final Sunday of helping at the farm Ben arrived home with a huge Christmas tree tied to the top of his car; he said Edwin had offered him one of the larger trees that had not sold as a thank you for his help. Adam and Ben carried it from the car into the hallway and between them hoisted it upstairs. I had cleared the chair from the turret bay window where it was going to stand in our apartment. But even as it came through the door into the lounge, we could see that it was going to be too tall for the turret-ceiling alcove.

As Adam stood the tree on its end, the top two feet were bending over at a right angle. 'What are we going to do about that?' I asked. Ben offered to tie the end branch down with some string, but Adam suggested finding the secateurs from the basement and lopping the top off.

While Ben disappeared downstairs to find them, we manoeuvred the fir tree into position. It stood full and proud except for the top two feet that bent over at a peculiar angle. We stood back and looked at the enormous tree – it filled the alcove with no room to spare. It would be a tight squeeze to decorate it and festoon the boughs with white flickering lights. 'Perhaps we should decorate it then put it up in the alcove?' I suggested.

To this we agreed, so between us we lifted the spruce back down into the living room. Adam pulled the tree over so that I could snip the top twenty-four inches off. The top bough fell to the floor as I cut into the stem leaving a stubby top to the tree. After forcing the bottom of the tree into the stand, we stood the huge spruce up into its vertical position and then all took a few steps back to admire our handiwork. Well, with the top missing we had completely ruined the shape of the spruce, and I was disappointed that we had mutilated such a fine specimen.

The large box of fairy lights was opened, and a long string of white pearls were unwound from the card they had been wrapped round. Adam suggested we plug them in to make sure they were working, as he did so, they flickered into a hundred little twinkling stars.

'All present and correct,' Ben said. We took turns passing the bundle of lights round the tree as we positioned them systematically throughout the branches. It required two sets of fairy lights, being so big, and twice as much tinsel as we had, but I volunteered to purchase a few more garlands to make it look festive and full. Adam brought the box of baubles up from the basement and we set to work decorating the topless spruce.

Age-old sentimental baubles, including a stained-glass, hand-made star given to me years ago by my school friend Chris and her husband, brought back lovely memories of the times we had spent staying with them down in St Just in Cornwall, and the lovely special clifftop walk we did from Land's End to Sennen Cove on that windy day back in the summer.

There was also the small clay finger-sized wedding jug we had purchased on a trip to New Mexico when we travelled there to see the home of Maria Martinez, a Native American potter. We had sat under the very tree where she had coiled her beautiful clay pots and jugs back in the 1920s.

Then there were the porcelain candy sticks our two sons had bought us when they were young and the fairy that had adorned every Christmas tree, we had ever decorated in our home back in Fairoaks. Unfortunately, she was going to sit rather uncomfortably this year on a hacked-off spruce due to the stubby top of our tree!

After an hour of decorating and rearranging all the festive bric-a-brac, we stood back to admire our handiwork. The tree looked slightly awkward and misshapen and slightly disappointing due to the mutilation it had undergone, but it was what it was, as Adam pointed out.

Our next task was to lift the whole ensemble between the three of us up on to the raised turret into the alcove where it would sit until the New Year. This proved to be very tricky as the weight of such a fine specimen was extremely heavy and the awkward handling of the tree caused us to be pricked and stabbed as we manoeuvred it into position.

Adam caught his breath as the whole tree nearly toppled over on one occasion and swore twice as his face was stabbed by the spiky branches, but eventually we manhandled the festive offering into its rightful space. Job done!

The day soon came when we were meeting up for the Christmas festivities down in the hall. I had spent the morning making snowflake shaped shortbread and was looking forward to dressing up in something a little Christmassy. Ben was home and had put on his Christmas jumper, the one I had purchased in TK Maxx as a joke last year. It had a large applique reindeer with a red nose that beeped when you squeezed it.

I was in the kitchen plating up the shortbread on a white Christmas doily when the doorbell rang. Ben answered the intercom and grinned it was Thomas. 'Thought I'd pop in for a pre-Christmas catch-up,' he said as he came up the stairs and through the front door. He commented on how festive the hall looked downstairs. The large thirty-foot fir tree in the hall had been chosen by Adam a week before and Felix had cut it down as promised and between the three of them, Adam, Felix and Jeremy had erected it in the corner of the great hall. It was going to look amazing after we had decorated it this evening. I knew Francesco and Lena had already put the white twinkling fairy lanterns on the tree and had insisted they would bring along all the trimmings required for the decorating of the spruce.

Adam came out of the bedroom when he heard Thomas's voice. He commented on the fact that Thomas was not due to join us until Christmas Eve but gave him a bear hug and wished him Merry Christmas anyway.

'We are just getting ready to go downstairs for a Battlefields Christmas get-together and a tree-decorating, punch-drinking, mince-pie-eating evening with our Battlefields neighbours,' Adam said.

I assured Thomas that it would be fine for him to join us in the festivities. He joked, 'Perhaps Ben will bring his guitar along for a carol sing-along.' Ben screwed up his nose and said how out of practice he was and anyway carols were just not his thing.

As I opened the door, we could hear movement down in the hallway and voices at the bottom of the stairway. The sound rose through the cantilevered spiral and sounded like someone humming the tune 'White Christmas'. This bought a co-ordinated sigh from Ben and Thomas; they clutched their hands to their hearts and wiped a little tear from their cheeks. All this was done tongue-in-cheek, of course! They laughed as they trotted down the stairs pushing each other as they went.

We entered the hall to find Francesco and Lena rummaging through several large boxes full of tissue paper. Lena pulled out several white porcelain doves with tiny feathers protruding from their tails and displayed them in little lines on the table. There must have been twenty at least all lined up like ducks at a fairground waiting to be shot down by an eager marksman.

She acknowledged us and asked if we could help unpack the other boxes of ornaments she had brought along, and as we obliged, she disappeared into her kitchen to fetch more boxes. On her return she stated that all these ornaments were brought from Germany where they had been used throughout her childhood to decorate her Christmas tree when she had been little.

It was also mentioned in passing that only white decorations were to be used on the tree this year. It was a good job that I had not brought down any of my red and green mismatched ornaments, as they would surely not have made the Lena grade of acceptance.

After bringing out several more boxes containing white ornaments of varying design, she proceeded to produce a large portable plug-in tabletop heating plate. This was going to be interesting, I thought.

She then disappeared into the kitchen once again and carried out a white ceramic tureen with a matching lid on top. From under the lid came a delicious aroma that you only ever smell at a certain time of the year – and that was Christmas. It smelt of warm cinnamon, honey and mulled wine. She lifted the lid and stooped down to take a breath of the concoction, and a faint smile passed her lips. She produced a tablespoon and proceeded to taste the warm liquid, licking her lips in a seductive way; she was in heaven!

Ben gave me a wry look. He too had noticed the secretive tasting and bent his head over the box he was rummaging through, trying hard not to laugh.

Suddenly from upstairs we heard a door click shut and

Cordelia appeared, coming down the stairs like a graceful swan gliding on a millpond. Now Cordelia was an unknown quantity as I had only met her face to face once, and that was by chance. I had followed her down the drive a few weeks ago and we had alighted from our cars at the same time in the car park. She stepped out gracefully with her two feet landing on the tarmac at the same time, as you would expect royalty to alight from a Rolls-Royce to avoid the unwanted tabloid photograph of an ungainly parting of the knees and a glimpse of a suspender belt or lacy knickers. I had seen it done to perfection by The Queen at Ascot, but never quite perfected the technique myself.

I had admired the procedure though from a distance and considered Cordelia to be quite a lady. Or so I thought, at the time!

Whenever I had seen her from a distance, she was always dressed to exquisite perfection – her clothes were expensive and could only have come from a Bath boutique, her luxurious high-heeled shoes always matching in colour co-ordination with her outfit. She had an endless supply of handbags, either in leather or animal skin, which swung over the crook of her elbow or were positioned perfectly over her shoulder swinging at waist height as she walked. During the summer months she often wore a pair of Jackie Kennedy sunglasses which looked very stylish. I always thought a headscarf was all she needed to be a JK lookalike. She mostly kept herself to herself but was always polite, nodding slightly or giving a little wave in acknowledgement.

It was interesting to see her come down into the hall and I hoped we could get to know her a little more. I approached her and introduced myself and my family. She chatted confidently to us all in turn, asking Ben if it was him that was the guitar player, as she often heard him through the partition wall that separated her lounge from his bedroom. Ben was not sure if she was complaining or complimenting him on his playing.

She spoke to Thomas next and expressed her approval of his car that she had seen in the car park, adding that she liked the colour. I was sure Thomas blushed slightly, but perhaps it was the fact that it was cold in the hallway, and his cheeks were rosy from the cool air. The thought raised my eyebrows. I thought Cordelia certainly had a way with the male species.

Then she spoke directly to me and apologised for not speaking sooner, but she was a private person, she explained. She then went on to tell us that she was having her apartment kitchen and lounge reconfigured and decorators would be coming in during January and February. Walls would be knocked down and workers would be coming up and down the stairs. She hoped it would not be too noisy for us and finished by saying that she would be away while this was going on. I enquired what she was having done and she went on to explain that the layout in her apartment was not to her liking and had been poorly thought out by the architect that had designed the interior. There would be new kitchen units, which she had chosen, and neutral colour schemes that she was introducing into each room. It sounded fantastic and I said I would love to see it when it was finished; she replied that I must come up for coffee before the renovations started and then again when they were finished. I hoped she remembered to keep her invitation open as I was hoping she might become another friend at Battlefields.

When Lena saw Cordelia, she nodded in recognition but never joined our group or talked to her. I wondered if they had fallen out in the past or whether Cordelia just was not Lena's cup of tea.

Eventually there was an end to the boxes and Francesco came from the apartment carrying a tray of home-made sliced *stollen*, followed by a plate of almond spritz cookies and Oma's *Apfelkuchen*, which Lena translated into English as *Grandma's apple cake*. There were also eight small ceramic mugs of non-alcoholic eggnog, which was a favourite recipe handed down through Lena's side of the family going back three Schneider generations. Lena must have spent two or three days preparing all these family recipes and took great pride in displaying them all on the white linen tablecloth.

With a creak the large white door to the right of the great hall opened and in came Felicity and Daniel from number four. Felicity was heavily pregnant with her first child and had come dressed for the festive occasion wearing a Mother Christmas outfit that rode up at the front due to the large baby bump now protruding from under the festive garment. She also sported a large red matching Santa hat. Daniel wore a similar hat but had not quite gone as far as Felicity in dressing the part of Father Christmas as he was wearing his usual jeans. But he did sport a red Christmas jumper complete with Rudolph's head and red nose. They gave a general wave and a 'Happy Christmas!' greeting went around the residents, everyone stood waiting expectantly for something to happen.

When everyone had laid out their festive offerings and Lena had inspected them, adjusting an odd plate or cracker to her liking on the table, Francesco plugged in a CD player in the corner of the hall next to the Christmas tree and pressed the ON button. 'Silent Night' suddenly belted out into the room making everyone jump. Francesco quickly adjusted the volume to a reasonable level and apologised to all those standing around.

At that moment we heard a car coming down the drive and then park up in the car park just outside. Helen and Michael jumped out of the car and hurried to the front door. I unlatched it before Helen found her key and pulled the great door open.

'Sorry to be late, but we got stuck in the traffic coming up from Bath,' Helen apologised.

Francesco and Lena, who seemed to be a little annoyed by their late arrival, turned their backs and continued to rearrange the glass cups on the table. Helen rushed past everyone and ran up the stairway two at a time, calling out as she went that she would only be a minute as she had some mince pies and some biscuits for the table.

The music had changed to 'We wish you a Merry Christmas' by then and Lena had started handing out small white plates to everyone.

Helen came rushing down the stairs, mince pies on a plate and biscuits still in the packet. Francesco gave Lena a nod and she walked over to the tree and switched off the hall lights, leaving us all in complete darkness. Then Francesco started counting backwards. 'Five, four, three, two one.' We heard a click and the Christmas tree lights twinkled, covering the enormous tree in hundreds of sparkling jewels. It looked amazing!

We were handed an array of white – and only white – decorations to hang on the spruce: the little white doves, large white snowballs hanging on white ribbon, white stars with glitter on silver threads and white tinsel that we were to hang. We did this with only the light from the tree to guide us, as the hall lights were switched off and would only go back on when the tree was fully dressed apparently.

This festooning went on for at least an hour and I could see Thomas and Ben were getting a little weary and were hoping for something to eat as it was past 8 p.m. Finally, every little ornament was in its place and Lena was allowed to switch the lights back on.

I noticed that Jeremy, Jessica, Felix and Madalyn had not joined us all in the hall and wondered where they were. It was not like them to stay away as they were quite sociable neighbours and I had become quite friendly with them all over the last year. Perhaps they were otherwise engaged but I was sure Jeremy and Jessica were in their apartment as their car was out by their garage, and they could not have gone anywhere without it.

Well, perhaps they were out with Felix and Madalyn I supposed, but it was a shame they were not here to join in the festivities. The evening had been organised by Francesco and Lena and the food and wine they had provided was delicious.

Everyone ate and chatted and the atmosphere was jovial and friendly, and the background music made us all feel that Christmas had arrived at Battlefields. My family was with me and our first Christmas was going to be exciting and different from any other in the past.

CHAPTER 12

THE HUMAN SNOWPLOUGH

In the middle of January, the temperature dropped suddenly taking everyone by surprise. There had been a few snow flurries on and off for a week or so and going out for walks became a cold, half-hearted affair. The weather forecast was predicting a long cold freeze with temperatures below minus one for the foreseeable future, but snow was not on the weather forecasters' menu, although it was certainly cold enough.

Frost covered the windows in entrance way downstairs and everyone was complaining to Adam that the radiators there were not giving out enough heat. It was, they said, 'as cold in the hallway as it was outside'. There was a draught coming through the wooden frame of the front door and several notes had been pushed under our door with various thoughts from the residents as to what should be done about it.

Felicity and Daniel, whose doorway was just off the main entrance, complained that this was the third Winter they had raised the issue with the management committee and still nothing had been done.

Adam sought guidance from Jeremy that afternoon, as

maintenance problems were usually undertaken by him, and he would be able to offer some sound advice. Jeremy explained to Adam, a little embarrassed by the mention of the draughts, that once again Walter and Francesco had talked the committee out of spending money over the years and the idea put forward to replace the oak doors was a cost that was too extravagant, and funding had been postponed until the situation improved..

Adam sent round a note to every resident stating that the situation would be resolved as quickly as possible, and he would purchase a roll of draught excluder from the local store and seal the gaps between the door and frame himself. This he did with Jeremy's help.

For the pricey sum of fifteen pounds, we bought enough excluder to surround the offending gaps round the oak doorframe, preventing any further complaints. We never produced the receipt or asked for reimbursement from treasurer Francesco, as Adam said he wouldn't bother as it was an insignificant sum. The problem had been resolved and there were 'far more important things to worry about,' he said. He also confided in me that after checking the radiators he had found them to be down on the lowest setting and so he'd turned the thermostat up in the hallway. If Francesco dared to mention it, he would tell him, as chairman, he had taken it upon himself to do it.

It was just as well we had sorted out the flow of cold air coming into the hallway as two days later there were a few snow flurries whirling around outside. At first it came down slowly, just a sprinkling like icing sugar over a chocolate Swiss roll at Christmas. But then overnight it came down quite hard and the grass disappeared under a few inches of the powdery white covering. It banked up along the grass verges and low snowdrifts were beginning to build around Battlefields. I thought it was enchanting and as it was the weekend it would probably be gone by Monday. Not so!

On Sunday morning, we awoke to a magical scene outside the window – overnight it had snowed a great deal. Snuggling up in our warm apartment on the first floor we had assumed the snow would slow and only the previous day's white covering would be left the following morning. We had assumed wrongly. Silently the snow had built up, laying down at least three feet of the powdery white stuff! I could see from the turret windows that the front door to the building was blocked with snow at least five feet high Even as a child I wished with all my heart that it would always snow at Christmas, and year after year I had always been disappointed that not all Christmases were white.

I raced down the hallway to Ben's bedroom where he was snuggled up under his thick duvet with only his mop of black curly hair sticking out. 'It's snowed, Ben – it's really deep out there!' A little muffled groan from somewhere under the bedding filtered out and his thick mop of hair disappeared further down as he pulled the quilt up over his head. I could not believe that this exciting news could be met with such indifference. I pulled at the quilt in the hope that he might at least be the slightest bit interested but he refused utterly to be engaged in conversation.

I left him, feeling slightly disappointed, and wandered into the kitchen to make a pot of tea for myself and Adam, who was still in bed with the duvet pulled up over his face too.

'Is it very deep?' he enquired, reluctantly peering out over the quilt edge and rubbing his eyes, when I took him in his cup of tea five minutes later. I wandered over to the window and took in the fantastic snowy scene outside. 'It is like a winter wonderland! it is absolutely beautiful and unspoilt by anyone' I said excitedly.

No one had so far ventured from the house and only a few rabbit tracks and deer hoofprints tracked across the white lawn and disappeared into the woods beyond the building. As I took in the wonderful view a deer came wandering from the thicket and slowly nuzzled at a patch of green by the edge of the lawn where a log lay. I stood bewitched by the scene from the window. I felt privileged to be there observing the animal as it fed confidently nuzzling at the few green shoots.

Adam stirred deep under the crumpled duvet, then a hand slowly drew back the bed covering and a bleary-eyed, hair-tousled husband appeared peeping over the bedclothes for the second time, rubbing his sleepy eyes.

'What time is it?' he inquired.

'I think it's time you got yourself out of bed and came and looked at this wonderful landscape before it all melts and vanishes like an Irish mist,' I laughed.

He pushed back the bedclothes and wandered over to where I stood surveying the view from the window. 'I think there's a draught coming from under the bedroom door, it's quite cold in here,' he said as he glanced over my shoulder and then gasped as he saw the wintry snowfall outside. 'Where did all that snow come from?' And in the next sentence he enquired as to how he would be able to get the car up the drive the following morning when he had to get to Newbury by 8 a.m.

I was so excited by the white paradise that it had not even

passed through my mind that tomorrow was Monday and Adam had an important international conference call scheduled with his American counterpart in the US the next day.

He swiftly pulled on his clothes and poked his head round Ben's bedroom door to see if he was awake. 'Ben,' I heard him shout. 'Ben, I need your help, buddy!' I could imagine the scene in the bedroom to be identical to the one I had just witnessed in my own room. A bleary-eyed, mop-haired copy of his father, Ben would not be overjoyed to be woken for a second time on his day off, but I knew after a hot cappuccino and a round of toast, he would be in more of a helpful frame of mind and would willingly assist his father in the snow-covered garden, to help clear the driveway

The two of them talked over the plan of action whilst munching on their breakfast. Adam was hoping that some of the residents might be available to help in clearing the lane down to the carpark, but he was unsure who was around. I knew Cordelia was not at home as she had gone to a gentleman friend's house and was not due back until the Tuesday. Even if she had been in residence, I really could not imagine Adam pushing a little notelet under her door inviting her to come and join in clearing the snow from the car park. I knew Francesco and Lena were at home as they had mentioned that her mother was coming for the New Year celebrations and Francesco had bought fireworks for the thirty-first of December, for a firework party in the garden, which he had invited us to. Felicity being pregnant was a non-starter and I knew Daniel was away for a few days, working.

But that did leave Jason and Jessica from number six, and Felix and Madalyn from the basement. As far as we knew Helen and Michael were in residence in number one, so they might be available as well.

As this discussion was taking place, we were all putting on several layers of clothing – thermal jumpers, thick woollen socks over a pair of cotton socks, lightweight body warmers outside our jumpers and our Polish coats, which had been tried and tested down to minus-four degrees the previous winter when we nearly froze to death on a visit to Warsaw. We had purchased lightweight bubble coats thickly insulated with a new technological revolution in thermal insulation. They had proved to be invaluable last winter in Poland, and we had left our thin anoraks behind in the hotel wardrobe with a paper sign pinned to the lapel of each coat saying, in Polish, '*dawac na cele charytatywne*' which translated meant 'give to charity'. We left hoping that this was the correct translation and guessed that two Polish homeless people would benefit from our cast-offs if the hotel followed our instructions.

Bundled up in this outdoor attire we headed down the stairway into the hall. There was deathly silence all around! Not a soul was up and out. We all looked at each other and Adam shrugged. 'Best we start as it's not going to clear itself,' he said.

After trudging along to the garage and brushing the snowdrift to one side with his wellington boot, Adam pulled up the garage door and handed us shovels and spades that hung from their brackets on twisted twine. We ploughed our way through the snowdrifts, which came up and over our wellington boots, the powdery white flakes finding their way down into the dry area of our socks and slowly melting as we walked.

We followed Adam to where the bottom of the winding

lane began and he stabbed the edge of the shovel into the snow, making a deep cut. The shovel stood upright on its own and we calculated that there was about eighteen inches covering the lane all the way to the top of the drive.

'Heck, this is going to take all day to clear,' he said. 'We need some help.' It was 10.30 a.m., and I wondered how we could attract the attention of our dear neighbours, hoping that they might feel a little guilty if they saw us struggling to clear such a vast area. After all, they would be using the driveway over the next few days. I made my way gingerly over to my car and finding the keys, switched on the engine. Adam and Ben wondered what I was doing, when suddenly I beeped the horn, a loud blast that echoed around the quiet countryside, bouncing off the distant hills. Ben cowered behind a tree, embarrassed that his own mother would do such a thing. Adam, knowing me, saw the funny side and clapped his ski-gloved hands together. 'That should wake them all up,' he said. We waited . . . Nothing!

Several minutes went by, but there was not a sound, still not a thing moved, no twitching curtains, no blinds drawn back out of curiosity, and no naked rumps from number four flitting across the ground-floor boudoir.

Adam picked up his shovel and started in earnest to part the snow on the drive. Ben and I helped as best as we could, shovelling and sweeping as we inched further up the lane.

It was hard back-breaking work, but we toiled on. We must have been shifting snow for at least an hour when from the bottom of the cellar steps emerged Felix, looking like Wally from the *Where's Wally?* book, the character who was in a red-striped jumper and red hat was hidden among hundreds of small, animated characters either working busily or walking across the pages of the highly coloured, pictorial book.

Felix had a thick, red-striped jumper on that was a little on the big side for him; under that a pair of red salopettes; on his head was a red, white and black striped bobble hat with two pom-poms on four-inch red strings, which circled his head, causing him to blink rapidly every time he nodded. His hands were clad in large black gauntlet-style gloves that came up to his elbows, like those used by welders when dealing with high-temperature joinery. He was a fine sight indeed. I do not think Ben could have looked him in the eye without laughing, but Adam was very keen to welcome a new recruit onboard and shook his thermal-lined, welder-gloved hand and thanked him for coming to help. Felix thought Jeremy would probably be out to help soon as he had lived through many a cold Winter here in Battlefields and had on many occasions found himself snowed in. He would have some good advice on the job in hand.

Within another twenty minutes Jeremy appeared from behind the oak front door. He was dressed in skiwear but an outfit that would have made Franz Klammer drool. He made his way towards us, grinning. 'Your first snow,' he said. 'It won't be your last.' He looked to where we had cleared the snow and stated that we had done well considering. We all set to work shovelling and shifting the powder and were in full swing when from behind the garages came Francesco. Dressed in a blue-and-white thermal onesie, large black fur-lined boots and matching gloves and black balaclava. Well, I guessed it was Francesco, but I could have been mistaken because all you could see were two large bulbous eyes and a pair of thick bushy eyebrows sticking out between the black face covering. I wondered to myself if he had previously used the balaclava in a bank robbery. I felt the air freeze as Jeremy stood up and saw him coming towards the group.

'You are starting from the wrong end!' shouted the black balaclava figure of Francesco. He pointed to the top of the drive. 'You should start at the top and work down towards the car park! Not work up the hill.'

Jeremy stood his ground. 'It makes no difference,' he said.

I could see there was going to be an incident, like two great stags locking horns. Adam really did not want to get involved with the debate, and Felix was 'quite happy', he said, to continue up the drive with his spade following his relative Jeremy.

Ben was watching the argument unfold leaning on his shovel. He was glad to take a break. I volunteered to get mugs of hot coffee and leftover Christmas cake, hoping to create a more pleasant atmosphere amongst our fellow shovellers and so slipped off to put the kettle on, leaving the stags to battle it out.

From the turret window on the first floor, I could see the debate was getting heated. Francesco stood in the middle of the group and hot air could be seen spewing forth from his nose and mouth in the cold atmosphere, like an international rugby scrum player on a frozen winter morning. Condensed steam was rising from the gathered group, and droplets of water came forth from their many flared nostrils, each giving their impassioned opinion as to which end of the drive they should start.

By the time I returned I could see the situation had finally resolved itself. Adam, Ben and Francesco were now at the top of the drive shovelling snow into heaps along the grass verge, working down towards the car park, while Felix and Jeremy were at the bottom of the drive shovelling snow and ice along the verge up the drive. I guessed Adam had intervened in the end and resolved the sticky situation by keeping the stags well apart in the park. I could see why Adam was so good at his job as a contract negotiator. The two separate groups slowly inched their way towards a common goal whilst keeping a safe distance apart. I was sure as time went on that the two groups were unconsciously shovelling faster and faster as they could see a middle ground between them open and each group was trying to prove they were fitter and more able than their counterparts at the other end of the drive.

Everyone occasionally glanced up to see if they were getting closer to the centre point on the curve of the driveway, and a few discussions were going on as to who would reach the bend first. I kept the shovellers sustained with mugs of tea, leftover mince pies and hot toddies, using up the rum given to Adam in the secret Santa at work. At the time of opening his Christmas gift from an unknown colleague, he had been dismayed to find it was rum (which he never drank) and puzzled by who would even think of giving him such a gift, suggesting at the time that the purchaser must have been looking to offload a previous secret Santa gift from the past.

The hot toddies must have taken a toll on the workers as I noticed from the turret window later that the two snow-ploughed lines were wavering a little and if they continued in their present direction, they might pass each other by without realising it!

As Jeremy and Felix neared the bend, they appeared to

be finding difficulty in clearing the ice as it was so thick, and discussions were made from both sides as to whether salt should be collected from the large council salt box that was half a mile away on the main road.

Ben and Adam volunteered to take the wheelbarrow off and, after locating the community salt box, would fill the wheelbarrow and return with a full load. This could then be spread over the stubborn icy area where the shade from the trees was allowing the ice under the snow to stay frozen solid.

Off they went while I retreated back into the warm apartment to thaw out my frozen fingers and toes. This left Francesco, Jeremy and Felix in a small group to talk among themselves, which did not last long. By the time I had removed my wellingtons, two pairs of thermal socks and had shaken the remnants of stowaway ice slivers that were clutching the sides of these woollen leg warmers, made myself a hot coffee and settled myself in the turret window, the group had disbanded. Each little figure had made its way through the snow to their own apartment doors and disappeared into the building, leaving a trail of meandering footprints in the white covering.

It was three and a half hours later that Adam and Ben came down the drive pushing a salt-laden wheelbarrow. It transpired that they had stopped to help a car that was having difficulty getting up the steep incline out on the main road and locating the salt box had proved more difficult than it seemed as it had been covered by a deep snowdrift.

Anyway, determined to finish the job, they spread the salty layer over the stubborn icy patches under the overhanging trees and came into the apartment shivering and red-faced. Ben went for a hot bath while Adam made himself a chocolate drink and wrapped himself in a warm blanket to thaw out, cuddling up to a heated water bottle that I popped on to his lap.

The drive was now clear for the following morning for Adam and any others to get to work. We had not seen any sign of Helen and Michael when clearing the snow on the Sunday, but the next day Adam noticed that when he went to his car, Michael's car had already left the car park, leaving a damp patch where the previous day his car had been parked under a mountain of snow. Adam was not impressed!

CHAPTER 13

RUN IT UP THE FLAGPOLE

The next management committee meeting was arranged for February and it happened to be convenient for everyone that it fell on the first. Helen and Michael had volunteered to hold the meeting in their apartment at the top of the building, stating that they had something important to discuss and it would be far easier to discuss it from number one. Adam and I were intrigued at this and wondered what it could possibly be, as up to now all meetings had been held at our apartment.

At 6.55 p.m. we climbed the spiral staircase, winding our way up, admiring the newly carpeted red river of woollen tuft as we went, and finally arrived at the entrance to their apartment and rang the brass doorbell.

After a minute or so the door opened and surprisingly Francesco's head peeped round the doorframe. 'Michael's just in the kitchen with Helen fixing some drinks,' he offered to our bewildered faces. 'They said to let you in.'

We were amazed to see Francesco as we had not heard any footfall going up the stairs past our apartment or had expected him to open the door to Helen and Michael's apartment.

Previously when Michael's 'patients', as he called them, made their way up to his apartment for one-to-one therapy, we heard them pass by. Peering on the odd occasion through the spyhole in the front door on hearing footsteps, to see who was visiting the upstairs apartment. I had seen many unfamiliar people making their way up the cantilever staircase. Michael had apologised in the past for their presence on the stairway and had spoken to us about the sensitivity of his work and the help he was providing to these unfortunate and anxious folk. He had stressed without reservation as to the importance of not conversing with these patients on any level when they were on the stairway.

This left us wondering about the type of therapy sessions Michael was offering and who his patients were. Up until now we had let it be, as we did not want to ruffle any feathers, being the newest residents to inhabit Battlefields House.

We had understood under the management committee rules and regulations that Battlefields was a residential building, and it was 'NOT PERMITTED FOR RESIDENTS TO RUN A BUSINESS FROM THEIR APARTMENTS'. It was stated in block capital letters, so why Michael was allowed to do so was a puzzle!

Another rule in the house was that it was 'NOT PERMITTED TO KEEP PETS!' As we had adhered to both stated rules, we were in two minds as to whether to raise the issue at the next meeting if we had concerns. Not all residents always attended these meetings – they were held on a too-regular basis for Adam. He would have been quite happy with a six-monthly or even annual get-together.

Trivial points or small issues were often raised, like: should we plant twenty daffodil bulbs or thirty in the border, and if we plant thirty should they be double daffodils, *poeticus* or *Tazetta daffodils*; should the garage doors be painted the same shade of green or could residents paint their garage door red if they wanted to; and should the tree that is leaning in the orchard be propped up with a wooden pole or should it be left to lean and fall over?

These issues irked Adam. He found the whole meeting process time-consuming and abrasive. Someone would always come up with an alternative to the most common-sense idea and it would go round and round the residential circle, until it would finally go to a vote. When three out of four times there would be no decisive result, Adam being chairman would have to cast his deciding vote and thus become either the hero or the villain. Francesco was the worst for this and made life very difficult for Adam if things did not go his way.

Adam was used to negotiating in his job but after a day's work he really did not look forward to these confrontations with the people he shared a building with.

Present at the meeting, in addition to the residents of numbers one and seven, were Daniel without Felicity, who was now looking after their new baby girl called Rosanna; Felix without Madalyn; Jeremy and Jessica and Adam and myself.

Adam started the meeting as usual and raised item number one on the agenda, which on this occasion was Michael's concern that had intrigued us all week. Adam handed the baton over to Michael and he stood up to make his point.

'For some time,' he said, 'I have been thinking that we should have a flagpole here at Battlefields House, complete with our own Battlefields flag.' We all sat quietly bemused while he continued to explain his thinking. 'We could erect a flagpole outside my apartment, and it could be attached to the original brackets that remain from a previous pole that had once fluttered over Battlefields House in the eighteenth century,' he said. He continued to say there could be a residents' competition to design the flag and the very flag chosen could flutter over the rooftops on special occasions once more. The special occasions being the birth of a Battlefields baby, the death of a resident or King Charles's official birthday,

As it was the first of April, I immediately thought it was an April fool joke and recalled a time when Adam was playing football for his usual team on a Saturday afternoon I had secretly unlaced his football boots and laced them back up with small brass bells interwoven between the laces, as an April fools joke. It was not until he got them out of his football bag and went to put them on that he noticed the bells. It was far too late to unlace them and lace them back up, so he played the first forty-five minutes of the match with his boots tinkling every time he ran or kicked the ball. It was not until half-time that he had the chance to re-tie his laces, removing the offending bells and shrugging off the banter from his team-mates. He never lived the event down, having picked up the nickname 'Jingle bells' ever after.

It transpired that Michael was entirely serious about his suggestion and I could see Adam rolling his eyes as he imagined the palaver about to unfold. Everything about the flagpole proposition had been thoroughly thought through by Michael – with Helen's approval – and it took us an hour to go through the whys and wherefores of the issue.

Michael insisted we all go out on to the battlement area to see the old fixings and the position where the flagpole would be attached to the turret on the tower. This involved us all, one by one climbing through the small casement window over the kitchen sink that was just within reach, if we climbed on to a small, upturned milk crate, provided by Helen. The window was not very big and while balancing on one leg you could just about get the other leg up and on the sill before clambering out on to the turret and the surrounding walkway. This was quite difficult, and Francesco needed a shove from behind as his back was a little stiff and he was not used to climbing through small windows, but with a few grunts and a push he got out.

From the ground level you could not see this area on the roof, but Michael and Helen had seen the advantage of the rooftop balcony and created a small terrace boarded out with wooden decking. It was perhaps ten feet in depth and traversed the small tower all the way round. With the sun shining in the right direction, they had created a lovely little private sun deck, unseen by anyone on the lower levels of Battlefields. What a bonus!

As we walked round the turret, which measured approximately thirty or forty yards in length, I could see the advantage of living on the top floor. Two sun-loungers with striped soft cushions stretched out on to the decking, complete with a small wooden table and two empty glasses that sat waiting patiently for their occupants to recline and enjoy the tranquillity of a sunny summer's afternoon.

It was a warm pleasant evening, with the sun going down, a magnificent view and the first star of the night twinkling on the horizon. I imagined Helen and Michael sat here in the quiet of the evening sipping a glass of wine and eating their Ritz biscuits with a dollop of Philadelphia on top, reclining on their stripy sunbeds while chaos reigned in the world below. Michael went on to explain the positioning of the pole, and how it would be a simple exercise to bolt the metal bracket holding the pole onto the wall, enabling the wooden shaft to slot in. After much discussion we all agreed for Helen and Michael to organise the project and gave them the go ahead.

After climbing rather awkwardly back in through the small window, knocking knees and bruising shins, we reorganised ourselves back in the apartment and voted to proceed with the flagpole idea and a competition would be held to design a flag that Battlefields residents would be proud of. Once again Battlefields would have its own flag fluttering over the battlements.

The rest of the meeting paled into insignificance as the excitement of the Battlefields quest to have its own flag was on everyone's mind. We set a date of 30 April as a deadline for entries to be submitted. There were no hard and fast rules about the design, but something appropriate for the building was agreed upon.

As it was Michael and Helen's 'baby' they would judge the competition, they said. This was the first bone of contention. Up until now Francesco had remained relatively quiet on the subject, but on the mention of judging, he felt that there should be an independent adjudicator.

Adam for once agreed with him on this and raised the question as to who that should be. Helen came back with the suggestion of their local vicar from the church they attended in Lansdown. He would be more than willing, she said, to step up to the challenge.

It was decided the vicar would do nicely and Helen said she would speak to him next Sunday after the service. Competition entries would remain anonymous and should be sealed in an A4 brown envelope with no writing whatsoever that would give a clue as to whose entry it was.

The next problem to solve was the actual flagpole on which the new flag would flutter. Jessica happened to mention that what she thought might be the original pole was down in the cellar, leaning against the wall at the far end. 'It can only have been there for a couple of hundred years,' she said, laughing. She occasionally went down to this area when she was putting the gardening equipment away and would get Jeremy and Felix to bring it up for inspection. She was willing to rub it down and remove the dirt and cobwebs from its surface and then residents could decide if it could be reused. We all agreed on this, and I told her I was happy to help.

Daniel suddenly piped up from his chair by the window. 'There is one problem that I can see,' he said thoughtfully. 'How are we going to get the flagpole up on to the roof?'

Everyone looked puzzled and gazed at him, hoping that he might come up with a solution. There were a few *mmmmmmms* and a few *aaaaaaaahs* and a lot of furrowed brows, until Adam suggested hoisting the pole with a winch to the rooftop. This was the only solution that anyone could think of, and once again Jeremy stepped in to offer his wisdom and commonsensical approach as to how this could be achieved. He could attach a winch to the four-by-four Range Rover and securing the pole to a rope, safely raise and manoeuvre it into position. We would have to attach a metal ring securely to one of the chimney breasts and thread the rope through it, thus creating an anchor point for the pulley system.

This all seemed plausible and, no one having a degree in science or engineering, we were all happy to let Jeremy organise the raising of the pole.

Adam breathed a sigh of relief when we finally got into bed that night. 'I think that went well,' he said quietly before he closed his eyes and drifted off to sleep.

A couple of weeks went by, and we heard that the vicar, who was called Reverend Simon Ainsley, was delighted to stand as judge for the flag-design competition and would come along on the thirtieth of April and make his decision on the winning design.

I had been busy thinking up ideas and doing some internet research into Battlefields House and Estate. My designs were based on flags I had seen in a Dartmoor college in a great hall hanging above the huge refectory tables where hundreds of students ate their lunches. We had stayed there for a few nights the previous summer while visiting the area, and I had taken photographs of them as I was interested in their patterns and unusual designs.

I was also interested in the history of the battle that had taken place in the local area in 1643 between the Royalists under Lord Hopton and the Parliamentarians under Sir William Waller. The Battle of Lansdown, I thought, might give me some inspiration.

After many days and tens of screwed-up A4 sheets of paper, I finally settled on a seventeenth-century cannon and a pile of cannon balls stacked in a triangular pattern for my chosen submission.

The design would be a gold silhouette of a seventeenth-century cannon set against a black background. I thought a piped red edge to the flag as a border would set the design off rather well. I drew and painted my entry carefully and on the thirtieth of April I headed down to the hallway to leave my entry on the large wooden sideboard, as arranged, in a large sealed, A4 brown paper envelope.

It was two o'clock and the Reverend Ainsley would be joining us at Battlefields at three o'clock to judge the competition. There were already three large brown envelopes on the sideboard, so I placed mine on top. *Fingers crossed*, I thought. I left the hall and returned upstairs to make a cup of tea for myself.

Sitting in the turret window sipping my tea, I wondered who else had entered the competition. It had been a great idea, and I hoped our neighbours might get together in the future and suggest ways of working towards a common goal and improving the community spirit.

By the time I had finished my tea Ben and Adam were back from playing golf. Ben, having won again and in good spirits, was keen to join us in the hall to hear the results of the competition. We all went down together to where a small gathering of residents was milling about, chatting amongst themselves.

A black saloon car came down the drive and pulled up rather sharply in the car park next to the lawn. Out stepped the Reverend in full cassock and shiny black shoes. We all watched as he stood for a moment in the carpark. It looked as if he had just come from a funeral service or reading the banns for a wedding ceremony. He was a tall, thin man with a comb-over hairstyle flapped slightly in the wind, and he had thick, round glasses and a bit of a stoop. He removed his glasses as he came towards the front door and took from his pocket a tissue that he then used to wipe the lenses of his spectacles vigorously.

He came through the open doorway and looked around at the expectant group of people. The residents who had entered the competition were gathered and Michael stepped forward and put out his hand to greet the visitor. 'Reverend,' he said, greeting the stranger like an old acquaintance.

Michael introduced the vicar to everyone in turn and offered him a glass of wine, which he drank a little too quickly for a vicar. He gave a little hiccup and put his finger to his lips and smiled, a little embarrassed by the misdemeanour.

He was taken over to the sideboard and Helen took the pile of large brown envelopes and handed them to him.

There were no chairs in the hallway, so he sat himself on the bottom of the stairs and thumbed open the first envelope. Francesco disappeared into the cellar and came back with a chair and offered it to the vicar, which he thanked him for.

The Reverend opened each envelope in turn, creating a nice, neat pile on his lap and we all strained over to see each other's entries, but he held them to his chest like a schoolboy hiding his work in an exam just in case someone was trying to copy his answers.

'Why don't you spread them out on the sideboard?' suggested Helen.

Reverend Simon thought this was a good idea as spreading them out on the floor to view the entries, he felt, would give him get neck-ache. I wondered why no one had brought a table for the competition entries to be spread on. It all seemed like a last-minute thought.

There were six entries altogether and as the vicar spread them out one by one carefully, I could see there had been a lot of thought over designs and each one had been carefully drawn and painted or coloured with different media. I tried to guess which flag design had been entered by which couple but found that almost impossible.

Michael offered the Reverend a second glass of wine, which he graciously accepted and after drinking the red wine even more quickly than the first, he bent over and continued to peruse the A4 sheets.

We stood in a semicircle round the Reverend, who was in the middle bending over, scrutinising the designs on the sideboard, when someone walked up to the front door, which was open at the time. The person stood quietly surveying the scene before him, whether he thought we were all in prayer or what I was not sure, but he bowed his head and clasped his hands together as if in respect for the group before him. I left the group and walked over to him, asking in a whisper what he wanted.

'Sorry,' he said apologetically. 'Has somebody passed away?'

Looking over towards the circled group with the vicar in the middle, all heads bowed, I could see the funny side of the situation. I assured the visitor that there had not been a death at Battlefields, and we were in the middle of making a decision on which design had won the flag competition.

He looked at me in a quizzical manner, then passed me a parcel and explained it was for the cottage up the drive but no one was in. Would I mind taking it for them, as there was a huge dog on the chain in the front garden and it was barking fiercely, and he really did not want to enter the premises to leave the brown paper package.

I took the parcel and assured him I would pass it on when there was someone home. With that he bowed his head, walked backwards and retreated up the drive.

It took twenty minutes for Reverend Ainsley to come to his decision. He then suddenly held up the design he had chosen. 'I would like to pronounce that this is the winner of the Battlefields flag competition,' he said, showing the A4 piece of artwork to the surrounding group. It was an image of a gold shield with two red pikes criss-crossing the shield through the centre and a capital B on the top of the shield and the letter H below. It was stylish and simple, and I thought it was worthy of the first position.

A round of applause went round the group, and it was Helen who stepped forward to shake the hand of the Reverend Simon Ainsley, who was smiling broadly. 'Well done,' he said, 'A marvellous design.'

Michael stepped up on to the first stair and congratulated his wife warmly, giving her a firm hug.

The competition now over, the vicar made his way to the front door, meandering a little under the influence of the two glasses of red wine he had consumed. He drove up the lane, knocking over a pot of hydrangeas sitting on the edge of the grass as he went.

Michael thanked everyone for taking part in the competition and assured the group that Helen would make the flag herself to save on costs. Apparently, she already had a piece of white canvas that would be perfect for the flag, and she would start immediately on the design.

Francesco mentioned the fact that we still had no flagpole *in situ* and asked where it was and when it would be erected. Jessica said that she had cleaned off the flagpole, sanded it down and it had already received its second coat of white exterior gloss. Having been in the cellar for hundreds of years it had been in a poorer condition than previously thought. But after a bit of restoration, it should be ready by the time Helen had finished making the newly chosen designed flag.

We would all be informed when the pole could be winched into position as it would require at least four or five people to help with the venture. This seemed to satisfy Francesco, who was a little annoyed that Helen had won the competition and was now looking to vent his frustration on somebody, and Jessica was often the target.

A week went by before we heard any news on the flagpole or flag, but one morning while collecting the post from the sideboard in the hall, I bumped into Jeremy who, attired in green overalls, wellington boots and a cap set at a jaunty angle, was just setting out to mow the lawn. He told me that the flagpole was ready at any time and could Adam arrange for a work party to get together and hoist the pole up to the top of the building. He explained that he and Michael had already attached two sturdy brackets to the turret in readiness for the pole to be winched into position. He said the brackets were strong enough to withstand a typhoon and would firmly hold the pole in place for years to come.

Speaking to Adam that evening, after he had spent several minutes admiring the stripes in the newly mown grass from the turret window, he suggested that we arrange the group to meet the following Saturday morning, weather permitting, and get the flagpole up and attached ready for the great unfurling.

'That would be one thing off the agenda at the next management meeting; one less thing to worry about,' he said.

Saturday came and as arranged a group of six willing participants gathered in the car park. Jason and Jessica had already carried the thirty-foot white gloss pole out into the car park and into the sunshine and the winch had been attached to their four-by-four. Michael had gone up on to the roof and was leaning precariously over the wall surrounding his apartment watching the proceedings below from the turret as we heaved the pole into an upright position.

Francesco had not yet emerged from his flat, so things were running quite smoothly. We were just pondering how to get the towrope up to Michael when Francesco came out of the front door. He was annoyed that no one had informed him that we were ready and waiting in the car park, and it was lucky he had seen Jessica and Jeremy carrying the pole from the garage earlier, otherwise, he said, he would not have been around to give his advice on how we should proceed.

Jeremy looked him up and down and gave him a stare but bit his lower lip and gave Jessica a look that said, *here we go again.*

Francesco went over to the upright wooden post that was leaning against the wall and scrutinised every inch that he could see up to five feet, ten inches, which was his height in full. He obviously could not find anything to complain about and gave a little '*Hurrumph*' like a baby elephant who might be trying to get his mother's attention.

A rope was needed to attach the pole to a pulley system, which then needed to be attached to the towing rope, or something like that, (my understanding of how the system was going to work was limited) but Jeremy seemed to know how the ropes should be attached and was obviously well qualified in these things.

Adam was happy to let him organise the job in hand and stood back, but Francesco always needed to interfere, even when things were going smoothly. He made suggestions and pointed out how things could and should be done. His presence just got under everyone's skin, even mine! It was finally suggested by Adam that Francesco should take the rope up to Michael and then after running the rope through the pulley system, he should throw it down to the car park so Jeremy could then attach it to the pole. This he did – at least it got him up and away from the rest of the residents in the car park.

We proceeded under the watchful eye of Jeremy and after the rope was thrown down from the turret it was attached to the pole, and he gave the go-ahead for the winch to be tightened. Jessica started the engine in the Range Rover, and it roared into life like a caged tiger ready to pounce on an unwary prey. Slowly the winch turned and we released the pole from our grasp. It inched its way up the granite wall, occasionally knocking the side as it climbed slowly onward. We could hear Francesco shouting from above, giving incoherent instructions, but we chose to ignore his rantings.

Finally, after fifteen minutes, the white flagpole was at the top of the building and Michael and Francesco stretched over to reach the end of the wooden lance and heaved it over the battlements. Job done!

At Adam's suggestion, we filed up the spiral stairway all the way to number one, where we could hear Michael shouting at the top of his voice that he needed help. Adam was the first to get to the small window and called that we were all here and ready to help. One by one we climbed up and through the small opening, heaving and pulling each other as we squeezed our way on to the turret and small gangway that led to the front of the building.

Michael was leaning over the parapet holding on to one end of the pole while Francesco was holding on to Michael by the belt of his trousers. Apparently, the pole's weight had tilted slightly after the rope had been detached and it was balancing precariously over the crenellations.

Adam put out his arm as far as he could and caught hold of the pole, swinging it back towards the building. Between the three of them they righted the flagpole and stood it against the wall with a sigh of relief.

We all stood in a line along the decking, looking out over the countryside. What a view we had from up here! You could see for miles around in every direction. We were above the tops of the trees and could view Bristol and even over to the Welsh countryside and the two bridges that spanned the River Severn. Quite magnificent. It was a shame that only Helen and Michael had access to this little piece of paradise on the roof.

Adam suggested manoeuvring the pole into position before we had any more problems and everyone agreed. It took three of the men to hoist it upright and into the correct position before it was secured against the wall and safely clipped into the metal brackets.

Helen reminded us, calling from the small window, that she had the flag ready to attach to the pole. She even had the rope and heavy-duty snap-hook clips that held it in place and had fitted grommets to the finished flag. Very professional. It was made to last well into the future and would flutter happily on many significant occasions over the Battlefields ramparts.

Michael attached the unfurled roll of canvas and raised it up to the top of the pole, where it graciously unfurled and flapped out in the gentle breeze that coincidentally blew at that precise moment. Everyone clapped and Helen, leaning out of the window, wiped a little tear from her bespectacled eye. The mission had been fulfilled, and we all happily eased our way back into the dining room, congratulating each other as we made our way back down into our apartments.

The flag with the gold shield with the red cross rose on many occasions over many years and delighted the residents whenever it was flown on those special occasions.

CHAPTER 14

CAR BOOTY

At the next management committee meeting in May, held at our apartment, the first item on the agenda was raised by Cordelia, who for once had graced us with her presence. She had never turned up for any of the meetings in the last year at any of the other residents' apartments. The fact was that after all the noise created back in February with the comings and goings of workmen, painters and decorators that visited her apartment, radio blaring on the landing, banging and knocking, cigarette smoke filtering down the stairway (when we had been strictly instructed that smoking on the premises was banned) she hadn't fulfilled her promise of a coffee when everything was finished.

Anyway, Cordelia surprised us by suggested having a car-boot sale! Every one of the female residents, well, the three of us present, were not too keen as we had little to sell, having moved recently. Everything that was superfluous to our needs had either gone to charity, been given away to family or handed over to the local refuse amenity for the site attendants to peruse.

But surprisingly Daniel, from the quiet corner of the room, agreed that it was a good idea, as he had much from the cellar to dispose of, and taking it to the local refuse site would be very time-consuming and inconvenient as he only had a small car. He liked the notion of turfing everything out of his locked room in the cellar, clearing out the mountain of garden tools from the garage that he never seemed to need and offloading a library of books that he would never read now that they had a new baby in the apartment. Also, making some cash on the side appealed to him.

Francesco was delighted that the Battlefields financial pot could be replenished with the revenue from the car-parking fees, he planned to impose on the public for using the grounds at Battlefields to sell their goods. The notion went round the room with five of the male residents agreeing to the idea. Motion carried!

It was agreed that the car-boot sale should be arranged as soon as possible because the weather had improved lately, and we were having a warm sunny spell.

Two weeks went by and the chosen Saturday of the car-boot arrived. Previously I had photocopied an A4 piece of paper with the words in bold capital letters:

CAR BOOT SALE
BATTLEFIELDS HOUSE
SATURDAY 20 MAY, 2 p.m.
ENTRY £20 PER CAR
BUYERS 50p

Laminating every copy, I had visited every newsagent in the vicinity and posted on several telegraph poles a copy of the notice.

Others had helped by advertising on social media and passing the word on the local grapevine. We did not know how many cars would turn up or how many people would attend but things had been well organised by the residents prior to the big day.

On Saturday morning there was a buzz around the place and residents were up early, sorting out the prime locations for the sale. A line of wallpaper-paste tables, trestle tables and workbenches were organised outside the garages; they varied in height, breadth and condition. Several had seen better days. Jessica and Jeremy had a large table that was quite sturdy-looking and new, while Felix and Madalyn had several large cardboard boxes, each containing books and cooking utensils. The wrought-iron table usually situated outside their apartment was now hauled into use, piled high with plates, pictures and broken bits of jewellery, buttons and hair accessories. The last to set up their stall was Cordelia, who seemed to have the male species wrapped round her little finger when it came to fetching and carrying. Felix and Adam were helping her bring a variety of belongings from her flat. A huge portable clothes rail was winging its way down the stairway, supported at each end by a cheerful twosome, whistling as they went. I think it went 'Hi-Ho, Hi-Ho, it's off to work we go,' which was quite amusing to Jessica and me. Adam and Felix carried the loaded rail to where Cordelia motioned them to put it down at the end of her table, and off they went again to collect even more bric-a-brac for Her Ladyship.

Cordelia continued to sort through her clothing items, pulling each garment out and brushing a little speck of dust or thread of cotton from a sleeve or collar, humming to herself.

When Felix and Adam came back out of the building for

the third time, carrying a folding French dressing screen for Cordelia, Madalyn called Felix over and I heard her mention to him that there were still plenty of items to collect from the basement that needed bringing up for her. Obediently he set off in the direction of the cellar with his tail between his legs and Adam disappeared for a quick cup of tea with me following him closely.

After a drink and a bite to eat we went down to the cellar to see if there was anything else we could find that was worth selling. Adam pointed out the rickety old wooden ladder that had belonged to my father. It was leaning, folded up in the same position as the day it had been put there a year and a half earlier. It brought back memories of when, as a child, my three young siblings and I had carried it out of the garage and erected it in the back garden during the school summer holidays. We used it to dare each other into jumping off the top platform holding on to a bedsheet or an old umbrella, pretending we were parachuting or flying through the air like Mary Poppins.

Another pastime we had loved was placing a plank of wood supported by a stack of two bricks sitting one on top of the other in the garden. We pretended to be elite gymnasts competing in the Olympic games, balancing on one foot and trying to pirouette like a ballerina without falling off.

I laughed at the memory and told Adam that I could not let the ladder go. There were a few boxes of the boys' toys that I held on to, thinking that one day the box of red-and-white Lego bricks might come in useful if we had grandchildren. Also, the push-along spotty dog that wagged its tail and the multicoloured teddy bear with all the stuffing squeezed out of its left arm where

Thomas had held on to it as he slept when he was a toddler. No, these things would stay.

Adam put this arm round me and called me a softie, but some things you could not part with and were meant to stay with us forever!

Returning to the car park where Francesco, now dressed in hi-vis yellow jacket and holding an official-looking notepad, was pacing up and down talking to Jeremy. The two were in great debate as to where visitor cars should park, as the garage area would be taken up with vendors' cars and tables. Francesco was insisting that the lawn area down the bank towards the trees on the left was where people should be directed, and he was the one who would be directing them there.

Jeremy was concerned about the vehicles churning up the newly trimmed lawn and insisted that cars should be stopped at the top of the drive and directed to a pull-in car park up near the local Grenville monument, where it was convenient for parking. The public could then walk down the meandering lane to Battlefields minus their vehicles, but Francesco was having none of it.

He complained to Adam that people would not come if they had to park well up the road and then walk down. He also pointed out that he was hoping to take revenue for the cars coming in to park. If they charged two pounds per car, he estimated the lawn could accommodate at least thirty cars, bringing in sixty pounds, or more if they were double-parked.

Adam calmed the situation by pointing out that if we moved the tables on to the grassy lawn, the car park could be used for people who did not want to park out on the main road and walk down. If they wanted to use the garage area to park, then they could pay for the privilege.

The cars using their vehicles to sell from would have to drive over the lawn, there was no way round that. Both men were a little disgruntled and went off in different directions muttering under their breath, Francesco to the back of the house and Jeremy to the garages, where he disappeared out of sight.

Adam instructed the residents to move all the tables and all the items for sale over to the lawn near the front of the house. This was treated with *ohhhhs!* and *aaaahs!* by our neighbours who had been busy setting out their stalls. Nevertheless, wheelbarrows, trolleys and pulley were initiated to help move all the items to their new home on the lawn as it made sense!

It was amazing to see all the contents passing to their new location. Cordelia's rail of clothing was being pulled along across the lawn, bumping and swaying as it went, preceded by Cordelia, who was most annoyed at having to transport it herself this time. Bags of clothing, items from her old kitchen, plus rolls of leftover wallpaper and paint tins from her new kitchen venture went before my eyes. A few unopened tins of *Little Green Acorn* paint caught my eye as they passed by on a trolley. I made a mental note to peruse Cordelia's table before the public came along as I knew the National Trust had its own paint pallet and I quite fancied the Acorn shade for my bathroom, especially if it was satin. I began to wonder what other luxuries or concealed gems there might be hidden amongst all the items that were going on sale this afternoon.

It took hours for everyone to present their belongings and bric-a-brac in an order with which they were satisfied, and after much manoeuvring and titivating, most residents were rather pleased with their stalls. We all wandered over to one another's tables, discreetly eyeing the goodies on offer.

Cordelia had sauntered off to get a cup of tea from her apartment and had left her table unattended, leaving Jessica to keep an eye on things for her, she made a beeline for the big box of folded jumpers. After rummaging through, she held up a cashmere honey-coloured cardigan.

Very nice, I thought. I wondered how much Cordelia would ask for the garment and wandered over to peek at the jewellery on display. There was a nice double-stranded necklace that I thought was made of jade beads; I would ask her when she came back if she was happy to sell it to me.

Jeremy had returned by then and was lining up a few old spades that he had found in the derelict shed in the field they rented. His stall mainly consisted of garden implements, jars of screws and nails, and picture frames, some with paintings, some without pictures, and old flower pots. In the meantime, Jessica had been busy potting up lavender cuttings into little pots along with wild garlic that grew abundantly all around us under the trees and had arranged them neatly on her stall.

Francesco's stall was the most interesting. He had a variety of unusual items to sell. It reminded me of an antique shop combined with a charity shop. Beside the table on the grass was a huge green glass bottle three feet in height and a beautiful pear-drop shape. I would have loved to see the person who had blown it – he or she must have had an enormous pair of lungs. There was a camouflage all-in-one suit, draped with imitation ferns and greenery. I wondered when it had been used and if Francesco had been in the Italian territorial army once upon a time. Sitting on the table was a tin bucket with eight rolling pins with varying-coloured handles, a very nice porcelain cheese dome, two Tetley Tea Folk gift set mugs still in the box. There was also a sweet little round leaf-shaped plastic tray complete with five multicoloured egg cups, a very nice Betty Blue striped teapot, an unusual set of plastic sandwich flags in German and an old wooden towel rail amongst an array of other interesting items.

Lena was off viewing my table, which I had set up at the end of the row, so I could browse for as long as I liked without any interference.

The most unusual item I had to sell from my display was a framed set of football cards featuring fifty giveaway Woodbine cigarette collection cards. Each one featured a footballer in full team kit poised in action. It was an item Adam had brought with him when we were married, having been left to him by his grandfather Harold.

As a boy, Adam had been given the collection one by one on a weekly basis every time his grandfather had opened his allowance of one packet of cigarettes for the weekend. Even though Adam had never smoked and had hated the smell of smoke on his grandfather's clothes and his yellow, nicotine-stained index finger, he had kept the cards as a reminder of the good times they had had during his boyhood, when they went to see Bristol Rovers together on a Saturday afternoon. He remembered the kindness he was shown and the joy they had both felt when their team had scored, his grandfather having once jumped up and down, dropping his hot pasty all over the ground.

Adam had given the OK to sell the set at the car-boot sale because the boys had not wanted them and I really could envisage a montage of cigarette cards on the wall in our apartment. So, Adam suggested we sell them to the highest bidder and give the money raised to a cancer charity. I promised I would not sell them for less than their value, and we would send off a cheque to the local hospice after they were sold.

Felix had set up and was bringing a few more boxes of clothing, bed linen and a few items of crockery up to his stall. Madalyn had set up a second table covered with a red-and-white checked tablecloth. On it she had placed twenty little clear plastic beakers in a rectangular formation. I wondered what she was going to put in them, so I wandered over to talk to her.

Apparently, she had produced two gallons of home-made lemonade and forty lemon-flavoured cookies for this afternoon. She had been busy in her tiny kitchen in her windowless cellar for the last two days, baking and squeezing lemons. I was in awe of her and offered my help when she wanted to bring them up from the basement nearer the time of the opening of the car-boot sale. She was grateful and said she would let me know when I was required.

By one o'clock the stalls were ready and looked full and interesting. Approximately fifteen car-booters had turned up, meandering down the drive, where they were greeted by Francesco, who immediately directed them to join the row of tables on the lawn area. Each vehicle sat exactly five feet apart and set behind an invisible line, each one with open-mouthed gaping car boots, like carp gasping for air in an overstocked pond.

By 1.30 there were a few early bird car-booters hoping to

catch a bargain.. Francesco was not pleased at their early arrival as he had to postpone his sandwich and cup of tea. We had popped to our apartment earlier to have our lunch and were ready and eager to start the afternoon.

An old chap, probably in his seventies, came over and enquired how much we were asking for the set of football cards – he was obviously an antique dealer looking for a bargain. Adam said fifty pounds and the stall-gazer baulked at the price. After shaking his head and fingering his lower lip, he looked Adam directly in the eye and offered thirty pounds. Undeterred, Adam stuck out for the fifty pounds, explaining that it was a collector's item and worth at least that amount. He also went on to explain that any money taken would be going to charity.

The elderly man scratched his chin this time, and after a long delay finally rummaged in his pocket and pulled out a fifty-pound note. He handed it over and Adam grinned from ear to ear, as he passed over the framed cards. The old gent turned and walked off in the direction of Cordelia's table with the package under his arm.

Gradually more and more people started arriving on foot, some cutting down the grassy banks instead of following the arrows that Francesco had so painstakingly pinned to the trees, directing them to the garages where he was waiting to take fifty pence from each new arrival.

Madalyn was selling her cookies and lemonade and gave me a wave. Cordelia was busy holding up lingerie to the sun to show how translucent the lacy negligée really was to a young couple. She had sold the folding dressing screen to the elderly chap, who was now struggling to carry it to his car.

There was a buzz around Francesco's stall. Lena was handing over several items at a time – she had an endless supply of Waitrose carrier bags tucked away under the table and produced one every time she made a sale. I thought the buyers were thinking they had a bargain as it came gift-wrapped in a Waitrose carrier bag. What a sales technique! *No Lidl bags here*, I thought.

Helen and Michael had been late to set up and were now at the end of the line of cars, hastily pulling out objects from pre-sealed boxes. They had resisted joining in from the beginning but were now backtracking on their decision not to have a table at the sale. It was obvious that they were waiting to see how successful it was before committing themselves to emptying their cellar space. Now they were playing catch-up, and Helen was rushing to and from the house while Michael was unwrapping glassware and crockery and literally throwing it on their hastily erected paste table, hopefully to get it all out on display in time to attract the viewing public.

Helen crossed the lawn in front of me carrying what looked like a black ballot box. Almost running, she heaved it on to the table and dropped it with a loud bang. The box had a large slot in the top and a printed sign on the side; and looked very official.

Adam said, 'Do you think they kept that one back when they last helped out with the local council election?' I did wonder how they came to own such an item. The box was snapped up by the same guy that had purchased Cordelia's dressing screen. He was buying up anything that had a possible quirkiness or value to it.

More vendors arrived, which stirred Francesco into action yet again. He waved at the cars coming down the drive to attract their attention, and each vehicle was guided into line, just as Francesco ordained. He held a short ornate stick in his right hand and pointed each vehicle driver into its appropriate space, tapping the side of the vehicle when he was happy with its position, much to the disbelief and annoyance of the driver. He looked like an army sergeant pacing up and down inspecting the regiment before he gave the order to fall out. Using his self-appointed authoritative manner and his trusty baton that was now tucked tightly under his arm, he took charge of the situation with aplomb.

The afternoon went well. Francesco had taken over a hundred pounds in revenue on the car park, and the car-boot money had exceeded all expectations, amounting to more than £600. Cordelia had sold just about everything from her table, while the late-comers Helen and Michael, apart from the ballot box, had missed the rush of buyers and were carrying their belongings back to their cellar lock-up and into the vaults of Battlefields, looking a little disillusioned.

Francesco, bereft now no cars were arriving, was taking off his yellow vest and eating a much-needed sandwich, which he had missed out on earlier.

As the last of the car-booters packed up and left, we boxed up the few items left over and Adam folded the trestle table, leaning it against a tree. As the sun was still shining, we wandered over to the grassy bank and sat down on a woollen rug we had unsuccessfully tried to sell. We decided to sit and enjoy the warmth that the afternoon had to offer.

Felix and Madalyn wandered over and asked if they could join us, Madalyn bringing the remnants of the lemonade and a plateful of cookies that turned out to be delicious. She said she would let me have the recipe as it was a hand-me-down from her grandmother. I was delighted with her offer and said I would make some and let her try them to see if they stood up to her grandmother's bake.

It was eight o'clock before we finally went indoors. Having found Felix and Madalyn entertaining company and having finished off the lemonade and moved on to a very nice Barons de Rothchild Lafite Reserve produced from the cellar and a leftover Christmas box of Rick Stein Cornish *Charcuterie*, we made our way up to our apartment, leaving the picnic and trestle table to be cleared away in the morning. It had been a good day.

CHAPTER 15

LITTLE CRITTERS

While potting down by the new glasshouse on one summer afternoon, arranging a hanging basket on the bench, I heard Jessica call out my name. As I stood up, I could see her coming over the bank brandishing a bundle of bamboo canes. Jeremy followed carrying a similar bundle of canes. As they proceeded to pick their way through the stinging nettles, Jessica shouted that they had finally purchased the canes for the runner beans.

'What runner beans?' I called back. She waved them in the air excitedly. 'These!' she said, holding up her shoulder bag.

As they made their way down the embankment, sliding and stumbling as they came nearer, I recalled that she had mentioned earlier in the year that she intended to plant some unusual varieties of runner beans and now they had obviously arrived by post.

On reaching the greenhouse she pulled her straw bag off her shoulder and opened it for me to see the varieties of seed. I glanced at the colourful array of bean packets – *The Czar*, *Firestorm* and a climbing French bean called *Cobra* were inside. Having never grown a single bean or pea in my lifetime, I was interested as to how and where these multicoloured pearls should be planted. I knew from the past, as a child, I had picked the fruits of my father's labours from upright canes on his allotment. My elder sister would reach up to pick the topmost beans, bumping me on the head with her basket as she leant over, often done on purpose if I complained.

We were seconded on a regular basis to help weed, hoe, pick and water what seemed at the time a prairie of upturned soil. It was labour-intensive and our arms ached, and our little fingers became stained ruby-red with the juice running between our fingers, as we picked off the bright purple blackcurrant gems and put them into little buckets, before tipping them into Dad's large bucket.

We were allowed to run around the allotment chasing each other if we did enough picking, and there was always a treat hidden up in the old shed – a Kit-Kat and a drink of fizzy pop if Dad thought we had been good and helpful.

In the hot summer and only on a Saturday as we had no school, we were allowed to strip off to our navy knickers and run through the cold-water sprinkler at the end of the allotment, often squirting it at each other, squealing with excitement and in trepidation as the freezing water hit our thin bodies.

The three of us – or four if we had to take our smallest sibling with us – would walk all the way to the allotment, sitting in turn in the giant wheelbarrow as my father pushed it to the huge vegetable patch a good distance from our home. On the way back the barrow was full of potatoes, cabbage, muddy carrots and buckets of berries, so there was not enough room for a ride home and we had to walk. It seemed a long way at the time, when we were only eight or nine, but in hindsight it was only half a mile. Happy days!

Jeremy handed the beanpoles over and said he was off to the field they rented, where he was doing some much-needed pruning. He swatted at a buzzing insect as he climbed back up the bank.

We continued our conversation about the bean planting and Jessica suggested a good patch for the canes would be in a clearing away from the tree shade. We cleared an area, weeded it and turned it over, creating a rectangle of approximately fifteen by six feet. This, Jessica assured me, would be enough for ten bamboo canes either side. The beans were to be planted two inches deep and two beans to a cane. Jessica had done the research, read the instructions on the packet, and was on a bean-planting mission.

I was glad to help and learn something at the same time. *Who knows*, I thought. *I may even have a little patch myself down here next year if the planting proved successful.* French beans for Sunday lunch – my mother-in-law would be impressed. She had grown runner beans as long as I had known her, always picking a handful for us if we went down to visit on a Saturday lunchtime in the autumn.

Securing the canes with string-ties, we were just planting the beans when Jessica screeched. I looked up to see her holding her arm as a wasp flew off in an upward direction.

'Damn,' she said, 'I've been stung by a wasp!' She eyed the sting closely and decided she needed some antihistamine and antiseptic cream as the sting was beginning to burn. I told her I would finish the planting if she wanted to go back to her apartment. She hastened up the bank and disappeared, cursing she went. Jeremy followed her to check on the sting leaving me alone.

I finished popping the little seeds into their respective holes in the ground and tidied around the greenhouse. I would let Jessica know it was all done later. I had noticed a few wasps around lately and guessed it was the time of the year for wasp nest-building but hadn't given it much thought since.

As I wandered up the bank and across the car park, Helen and Michael were loading their Fiat 500 with cases. They were having trouble getting them in the small car, Helen forcing the cream-coloured suitcase into the boot while Michael was trying to close the passenger door after having placed a holdall in the footwell. I knew they were off on holiday, going down to Dorset to stay with Helen's sister for a week. She had a bungalow, and they often went this time of year to see her.

I stood and watched as they finally forced the boot closed. Helen looked up and I waved as they climbed into the car. They drove halfway up the drive, then suddenly screeched to a halt and the passenger door flew open. Helen jumped out, pulling at her hair like a frenzied madwoman. 'It's in my hair!' she was shouting, twisting and turning like an out-of-control spinning top, gyrating and squealing at the same time.

Michael exited the driver's door, running round to see if he could ease the traumatic situation that was unfolding. 'Stand still!' he shouted as she tore at her hair, shaking her head in an erratic manner.

'Has it gone? It was climbing on my head! Has it gone?' she wailed.

'Let me look; stand still, woman, and let me look!' Michael

grabbed Helen by the shoulders and bent her head forward. He peered at the top of her head and parted her hair, searching for a critter of some description. I heard Michael say, 'It is gone, whatever it was. It's gone.'

'I'm sure it was a wasp! A hornet! It was huge!' she protested.

'Did it sting you?' Michael asked.

'No, I don't think so, but it was crawling in my hair,' she whimpered.

'Well, it's gone now, honey; let's get back in the car,' Michael said patiently.

Helen ruffled her hair and gave a shiver, then gingerly climbed back into the vehicle, eyeing suspiciously the interior of the car before finally satisfying herself that there was no hiding monster of a wasp waiting to infest her hair once more.

They drove off up the lane on towards their week in the bungalow, with the car windows firmly shut!

I continued towards the main front door, noticing as I went a few buzzing insects congregating around the roses near the car park. I was a little concerned that there seemed too many for comfort and too much of a coincidence for that many wasps to be in the same area.

With that, Felix alighted from the underground cave he called home and gave me a friendly wave. I beckoned him over and met him halfway on the lawn. Explaining the wasp situation, I asked if he was aware of any nests in the garden. He was not but was happy to walk the perimeter of the building with me, so off we went.

The small orchard near the side of the house was buzzing with wasps, but we could see no obvious nesting site. As we neared the back of the building, Jeremy was coming up from his field and we explained the situation. He had noticed a lot of wasps around lately and told us that a few years ago they had found a large nest under an old haystack. It was huge and contained approximately 30,000 wasps according to the pest controller. They had decided to leave the site alone and let the nest's occupants die off naturally. If the nest was somewhere in the building, 'Well, that is another matter,' Jeremy said.

I told him Jessica had just been stung, and he said he would pop in to see her, but join us to hunt the nest down afterwards, as it needed to be identified quickly and dealt with one way or another. Felix said he would go down to the garages to have a look down there for any signs of a nest, so I continued round the building and not until I was back by the orchard, having circumnavigated Battlefields, did I notice a swarm of wasps buzzing around the balcony that hung out over Michael and Helen's top-floor window. I stood and watched as hundreds of the little critters came and went, in and out of a crack that roofed the balcony. They were coming and going like passengers alighting from a train at Paddington station.

Jeremy came back reporting that Jessica was having a sit-down, but she was all right. We continued to watch the wasps at work, gorging on the fermenting fruit that hung from the nearby trees and becoming intoxicated with apple juice. Apparently, they can become quite aggressive when drunk and will attack anything or anybody in the vicinity of the nest if disturbed.

Jeremy confirmed that we had located the nesting site and would set about contacting the pest controller he had previously used. He would call her out the following day to give us some advice. We arranged to meet up at ten a.m. and discuss the way forward.

The following day, promptly at nine fifty-five, the pest controller arrived in a small green van. Complete with full wasp protective all-in-one white cotton suit, she walked over to us carrying a large white mesh hood under her arm. Her smile was as wide as a crescent moon and her eyes a light blue, not quite what you might expect a pest controller to look like. She explained that she was the daughter of Trudy, the previous pest controller that had come out before and assured us that she was fully trained to advise and remove, if necessary, any offending nest.

Jeremy led us all towards the apple trees where the wasps were buzzing happily. She glanced up to where the insects were flying around Michael's balcony and appraised the situation quickly. She would need to get a closer look at the nesting site, as it appeared the actual papery nest was not in the roof but hanging under the balcony ceiling. Access would be needed to enter the balcony to inspect it properly, she said.

I explained that the residents were on holiday and would not be back for a week. At this explanation she suggested getting a tall ladder to scale to view the situation more closely from the outside.

Jeremy and Felix, who was happy to help, were on to it straight away! Off they marched down to the basement where the tallest ladder could be found. It was truly long and extended to three times the folded length and would easily reach the balcony.

After siting the lofty ladder Katie, as she became known, donned her mesh bonnet and scaled the dizzy heights to the balcony railings. She gingerly climbed the balustrade and disappeared from view. Within a few minutes she popped her head over the ironwork and shouted in a very excited voice that she had located the nest, and it was huge. I imagined the smile on her face at discovering such an exciting proposition.

It reminded me of a situation when another call-out was made to a service contractor when we had lived at Fairoaks. Our next-door neighbour Ernest had knocked on the front door and complained of a drain blockage – his toilet was not flushing properly. He was wondering if we had the same problem, and if we might be suffering in the same way.

It so happened that things were a little slow in that department and we shamefully admitted that our system we had been suffering a similar sluggishness for a few days. Our dear neighbours Mr and Mrs Barber had lived next to us quietly for fifteen years and were distressed at the situation that was developing and were not sure what to do.

At the time Adam, having the day off work, was hoping to find a golf partner for the afternoon. He did not really want to get embroiled in sorting out our neighbours' drain blockage and lacked the inclination to proceed any further. He was hoping the situation might resolve itself with a bottle of washing-up liquid poured down the toilet pan, a trick he had seen on YouTube as a quick fix for a stubborn log jam.

This not producing the desired effect caused him to 'TUT' rather loudly. I impressed on him that it would need to be sorted out as this type of problem only ever got worse. We would have to call out Dyno-Rod the blocked-drain specialist.

'It will cost a fortune!' Adam said, but Ernest, our worried neighbour, was willing to pay for the call-out if the blockage was in his pipework. Although we were having problems too, the obstruction might be in our pipework as our sewage pipes were connected in a line to the rest of the neighbours on our side of the cul-de-sac.

The phone call was made and the receptionist at Dyno-Rod assured us, after a deep and meaningful conversation about the problem, that an engineer would be with us within an hour as a priority call-out. We informed Mr and Mrs Barber, our neighbours to the right of us, what was happening, and they were very grateful.

Sure enough, forty minutes later, a van pulled up outside in the cul-de-sac. A bright young man in his twenties stood outside the front door rubbing his hands. I thought at the time that it was not cold but then I realised he was rubbing his hands in delightful anticipation of the task in hand.

'Run me through the problem,' he said with an excited voice, rubbing his hands once again as he listened to Adam talking him through the embarrassing situation.

He smiled at the end of the description of the problem and told us to leave it to him. He would find the blockage and resolve the sorry state of affairs. Our fat busting hero went out to the drain cover in the drive with us all following and lifted it with a special tool, pulling back the iron seal. He glanced into the drain, where he could see a build-up of what can only be described as BUILD UP!

I immediately stepped back from the opening along with Adam and retreated to a safer distance, out of the reach of the disgusting odour that seeped into our nostrils.

The young man, who was called Sam, glanced over and grimaced. 'This is a big job – probably a fat block,' he said. His face then broke into a smile and, rubbing his hands yet again, wandered off next door to ask Ernest if he could inspect their drain covering as well. We followed him at a safe distance.

'As I expected!' he said in such a way that you would have thought he had won the lottery not just discovered a blockage in a drainage system. 'It is backed up so the blockage must be further down the pipe, probably nearer the main road. 'This requires another member of the team to come out and help,' he said excitedly.

After phoning through to his head office and organising another expert to join in the hunt for the illusive fat blockage, he disappeared into his van and pulled out what looked like a long coil of rubber that had a sharp cutting device protruding from the end. He started to explain the complexities of clearing a drain that had back-up, telling us that when they found the fat jam, they would push this rubber hose down as far as the obstruction and rotate the nozzle to free the pipe and the flow of water that had built up back along the drainpipe.

It all sounded very technical and disgusting to us as drain-clearing novices, but he sounded like he knew what to do in this unfortunate chain of events.

An hour later another team member arrived, another Sam, and we could hear Sam number one explaining in exuberant terms what they needed to do. They would push the uncoiled tubing down the driveway drain outside our garage and see if it protruded into next door's drain. If it came through, they would know that the blockage was even further on down near the main road. That then became a major incident, and it would involve contacting the council to approve following the blockage into the main road, where it might be necessary to shut off the road to obtain an entry into the drain covering.

All this was very concerning. We were anxious about the cost and mentioned this to Sam number one, who assured us that this was a one-off payment that was usually covered by house insurance, or sometimes, if it was fatty deposit build-up, the neighbours all chipped in to the cost of unblocking the drain. But he added, 'If the main road drain has the blockage, it is down to the council to pay for the clearance.' A much better financial outcome for everyone.

He went back to work wriggling the rubber coil into the deep abyss, shouting to his team-mate Sam number two, to let him know when he spotted the end coming through. Suddenly we heard a shout. 'Got it!' came a voice from beyond the neighbour's fence.

Sam stopped feeding the coil and ran next door to inspect the drain entrance. He returned to inform us that the obstruction was further on down the line than he first thought and Sam number had not reached it yet. He would have to investigate the next-but-one neighbours' drain cover.

As the neighbours were not at home, he discovered after ringing their doorbell twice, he went on to their drive and opened the manhole cover. 'Eureka!' we heard him shout from a distance. He rushed back to tell us that he had located the ball of hard fat. His eyes lit up as he held out his arms, saying that it was 'this big'. He extended his arms and gave us a detailed description of a massive build-up of fatty deposit of the like that he had never seen before.

'Wait till I tell them back in the office,' he said, actually wringing his hands 'This must be a record!' he enthused.

His colleague was less enthusiastic about the size of the deposit and being new to the vocation was not so keen to get down in the drain and remove the large, disgusting, foul-smelling lump of encrusted fat build-up.

We retreated to the house until the episode was over, not wishing to partake in the celebrations that were going on between Sam and his office colleagues over the phone. It was a memory that stayed with me until this day. From that day onwards, no cooking fat went down my sink ever again.

Back up on the veranda of number one, Katie was returning from the balcony, steadily working her way back down the long ladder. Felix helped her off the last rung as she turned and sighed. 'I'm afraid I shall have to remove the nest, which means destroying it,' she said, sounding a little forlorn. 'We try to leave the wasps alone to let nature take its course, but in situations like this, we will treat the nest with chemicals and remove the nest a few days later when the wasps are eradicated.'

The cost involved would be one hundred pounds We agreed to this and off she went to mix the chemicals necessary for the process. She insisted we clear the vicinity, as breathing in any elements may cause vomiting or sore eyes.

We left her to continue with the extermination and it was an hour later that we saw her peeling off her breathing apparatus and packing away her equipment by the van, and we knew the dirty deed had been done.

Adam received an invoice a week later in the post and passed it on to Francesco to pay. Helen and Michael were delighted at the news of the removal of the nest when they got back from their vacation, as they had been wondering what to do about it!

CHAPTER 16

BRIGHT IDEA

While Michael and Helen were on their holiday in sunny Devon for the week, I had received a brochure in the post advertising an unusual offer. It was a drone company selling aerial photographic views of your home. Now this, I thought, would be an original idea for Adam's birthday coming up in early September.

I discussed it with Ben and Thomas and they offered to contribute to the cost of a drone flight and a large, framed photograph of Battlefields from the air. It would adorn our apartment wall and be a topic of interest when friends and relatives came to call. The painting and decorating had been finished earlier in the year, and we had one wall that was perfect for a large print.

This was an amazing idea and Ben and Thomas were very excited about the suggestion. Adam would love it!

I contacted the drone company, which turned out to be a single operator running a one-man show. He was very polite over the phone and could come out the following week to fly the drone over the property, taking several angles including a 500-foot-high view that encompassed the surrounding countryside. It sounded exactly what I wanted – It would be a unique present and we could not wait for Adam's birthday to present it to him.

We had also planned to have a special celebratory party on the lawn, hiring a marquee, chairs and tables and a caterer to provide all the food necessary for the guests to enjoy a wonderful afternoon.

I mentioned the drone flight and photograph for Adam birthday present to almost everyone at Battlefields and they thought it was a wonderful idea – even Francesco would be interested in seeing the photograph when we had it delivered. Unfortunately, Helen and Michael were away visiting relatives and would therefore be informed when they got back, but Jessica was sure they would not raise an objection. 'It might be nice to have a large print framed up for the hallway if funds allowed,' she suggested.

Adam's birthday was in a few weeks, so there was a lot to organise. It was arranged for the drone-pilot to come out while Adam was at work. Without him knowing, we had planned for the photographic flight on a Tuesday afternoon, as many of our neighbours were working or otherwise engaged and Tuesday always seemed to be the quietest day of the week.

I knew Francesco and Lena were away on holiday, Jeremy and Jessica would be down on their smallholding, and Michael and Helen were usually out on Tuesdays, involved with church business, although I had noticed their car was still in the car park. I hesitated as to whether to inform them that the drone would be flying over the Battlefields rooftop as I had not seen them to let them know but then was distracted as the drone pilot's car was coming down the drive.

He parked up and jumped out of his vehicle. I wandered over and introduced myself. He was a young man of approximately twenty-five years of age, and he went on to tell me he had started the business only a year ago. He had always been interested in drones and a keen photographer and, with a little inheritance money he had been left by his grandfather, he had indulged his passion and bought a drone. 'The business has literally taken off!' he laughed, adding that he was finding it difficult to keep up with demand. It seemed that every man and his dog wanted an aerial photograph of their humble abode.

We discussed terms and requirements, and he hastened to the back of the van to organise the drone. It was all very exciting and I could not wait to see the photograph and the surprise on Adam's face on his birthday.

The day was extremely hot, with little wind, so it was perfect for the flight, I hoped it would continue right up to Adam's birthday.

Philip, as I found out, was enthusiastic and very excitable when he brought the drone out for me to see. It was like a giant insect, black and shiny with propellers on four corners. He said he would do the first shot from high above Battlefields, then fly over taking several photographs from different angles at varying heights; it would only take fifteen minutes. He told me that if I wanted to be in the shot, I could walk over to the lawn area and look up, and he would be sure to pinpoint me in the picture. It was a brilliant idea, especially as it would be a lasting memory of our time living here at Battlefields.

The drone slowly rose high up into the air, hovering as it went, its four propellers spinning madly, making a quiet buzzing noise like a giant bumble bee. It soared and loitered over the rooftop, clicking and photographing as it went.

Philip moved around the garden, watching closely as it captured every angle of the medieval building. It was quite a sight as it flew overhead. I waved, hoping that Philip might capture me in the photograph.

After fifteen minutes the remotely piloted aircraft landed safely on the grass, having taken all the photographs necessary. Philip said that he would send an email with an attachment of the best shots, and I could pick out the one I liked the most. He would then get it blown up to A1 size and framed in plenty of time for Adam's birthday on the third of September.

CHAPTER 17

CELEBRATIONS

The party plans were coming together finally. Our family, Battlefield residents and friends were all joining us at twelve p.m. for party games on the lawn, music and afternoon tea. We were expecting fifty people to attend and had received acknowledgements in the post from everyone.

I was pleased to hear that Phyllis was able to come and had organised a taxi to bring her up and take her home again afterwards. She had enjoyed using the taxi when she visited previously and had got quite friendly with the taxi cabbie and had wondered why she had not used the service before. Not being short of a penny, I wondered too. It would be good to see her again.

I recalled the times over a cup of Earl Grey (her favourite tea) when she had reminisced about her life with her husband Jack and the time she had lived in California. Her life had been very different then. Her daughter Margaret had married a Hollywood producer and had a home on the beach in Malibu overlooking the Pacific Ocean. She told me of the white sandy beaches, the tall swaying palm trees and the exclusive boulevards where they went shopping together.

Jack and Phyllis had been part of the Hollywood scene in their younger years. I recall her telling me of the Tuesday afternoons when she played poker with Margaret and Nancy Sinatra, the wife of Frank Sinatra, by the pool, the lavish parties and the gorgeous gowns they wore to expensive restaurants in uptown Los Angeles. The time she sat next to Bill Bixby the actor who played the Incredible Hulk at a gala evening. There was even a black-and-white photograph of herself and Margaret standing either side of John Wayne the Hollywood actor, with his arms round them, all smiling into the camera lens.

She had endless photographs to show me, which she kept in a cardboard box in her wardrobe, of the people she had once known a lifetime ago.

Phyllis had come up to visit a few months ago months previously when she caught a lift with a friend, filling me in with all the local gossip that she loved to pass on. We had shared tales of her life over the years and recalled the time when out of the blue she had received a letter in the post containing a first-class return ticket to America from her daughter Margaret, who still lived in California.

To celebrate Phyllis's ninetieth birthday her daughter had organised a surprise trip over to stay with her for a month in Malibu. She amazed us by saying that she was going – flying from Heathrow Airport across the Atlantic Ocean to Los Angeles on her own, where she would holiday in the Californian sunshine once again with Margaret.

She had the time of her life and enjoyed every minute of her vacation. She even encouraged us to take a holiday to California to see for ourselves what an amazing state it was.

We visited several times after that, visiting the West Coast, cruising down the Pacific Coast Highway in an open-top Mustang with 'California Girls' by the Beach Boys blaring out from the radio. We tasted a little of California thanks to the tales of Phyllis and her insistence that we went. She said, 'Travel while you can, see the world and enjoy it; make memories of your own, as they're all you've got when you are old.' Phyllis always had a way with words!

Just before Adam's birthday, an email came through from Philip the drone owner. Attached to the email were six small images of the sky view of Battlefields House. Every one of them was amazing, but I particularly liked the shot where I could be seen waving far away on the lawn. It was my favourite, as I thought Adam might like the image of me in the picture as a way of remembering our time at our unusual home.

I emailed back straight away and received a message from Philip stating that the image would be enlarged to the A1 size we had agreed on, framed, and delivered on the second of September, the day before Adam's birthday.

True to his word the picture arrived. On returning home from shopping on Friday, the framed image was waiting for me in the hallway. I was sorry to have missed Philip as I had hoped to view the photograph with him, but time was not on my side. Adam was due home from work any moment, so I picked up the brown paper package tied tightly with red-and-white string and hurried down to the basement where I locked the picture in our cellar cupboard, hoping to view it later if I could sneak away from Adam.

As it transpired, I was unable to venture down to view

the package without causing suspicion so decided to leave it wrapped and would present it to Adam at the party as a surprise on the day, still in its original wrapping.

CHAPTER 18

PICTURE PERFECT

The morning of the party Thomas arrived early. He was as excited as we were about the festivities and, not having seen his relatives for a while, was looking forward to involving everybody in the party games he and Ben were organising. There would be apple-bobbing in the orchard, egg and spoon races for the adults, obstacle courses to navigate and guess the amount of jelly beans in the jar for the children.

I was looking forward to catching up with our dear friends, Chris and Rick and their two children, Matt and Rowan, who were coming up from Cornwall especially for the party. It had been nearly two years since we had seen them, as they had moved to St Just and had not been able to visit until now.

At nine a.m. the marquee company van rolled down the drive, parking in the car park. The driver jumped out of the vehicle and came over. We discussed where the marquee should be sited and agreed it would be best situated down at the far end of the garden, down the two slopes in front of the woods. Even though this was quite a way from the car park, the van driver did not seem to be too worried about the distance. The three employees, all in their teens, looked strong and agile and seemed quite jovial about the job in hand. They joked and teased each other, speaking in what I thought was Polish. I guessed they were hired help for the day.

The white tenting was loaded on to trollies and pulleys, the boxes full of ropes and pegs wheeled down the embankment all the way to the erection site. It took them well over two hours to erect the marquee, carrying matting for the interior, a wooden slatted dance floor that needed to be slotted together, and all the swags and tails to make the interior special.

Next it was the lighting and a generator that had to be connected to the mains, and that needed an extension cable to be run from the house. There was much to do but between the laughter and banter – none of which we could understand – things were going well.

I offered to get the guys sandwiches and drinks, which they were delighted about, so I retreated to the apartment, glad to get out of the heat for a while. While waiting for the kettle to boil, as I was desperate for a cup of tea, I glanced out of the turret window to see three heavy wooden six-foot-in-diameter round tables cartwheeling over the newly mown lawn and rolling down the hill towards the woods where, one after another, they bounced down the embankment, ricocheted off the trees before crashing into the woods or recoiling on to the grass, where one continued to spin like a penny before settling itself on the lawn.

I was horrified as, from where I was standing, I could see deep ruts carved in the grass like tramlines on a San Francisco transport network, cutting deeply into the beautifully manicured turf that Jeremy and Jessica had so lovingly prepared for the party.

The three lads were preparing another three round tables for their journey down the slope when, from out of the main front door, Francesco came running at full pelt. He made a beeline for the youths, shouting at the top of his voice for them to stop. But it was too late as three more heavy wooden discs hurtled past him, almost knocking him off his feet. He jumped out of the way just in time to see them freewheel into the distance, bouncing down into the trees.

The three youths stood looking at the six wooden platters lying like scattered tiddly winks in the distance. Then they looked at the red face of Francesco and it seemed to dawn on them that this was not good. '*Niedobrze?*' the youngest of the three said.

'*Niedobrze!*' shouted Francesco, seeming to understand the meaning behind the Polish word. He was about to blow his top when Adam came round from the garage to see what all the commotion was about. From where I was cowering behind the curtain, high up in the turret window, I could see Adam trying to calm the situation down. I heard the words, 'Sue for damage!' coming from Francesco as Adam tried to restore some form of tranquillity. Francesco threw his hands up in the air and stormed off in the direction of his apartment, obviously annoyed and seething at the situation and unable to contain himself any longer. I doubted if he would come to the party this afternoon. *Better that he goes to lie down in a dark, quiet room until his blood pressure restores itself to a normal level*, I thought.

Adam turned to the three youths and was obviously explaining that the tables should have been carried, not sent spinning out of control. This they seemed to understand and the eldest of the group was holding out his hands in an apologetic manner. It was too late to do anything about it now and the ruts in the lawn would have to be rolled and flattened after the party. I suspected Adam would lend a hand in overseeing this later. Other than this the afternoon arrangements were going well.

Thomas and Ben had been down to the cellar and found a large empty barrel that had lain there for years. Filling it with water from the outside tap, they had picked a dozen apples off the trees and the fruits were now bobbing up and down in the water.

Lines of powdered chalk had been laid down in running lanes at the bottom of the lawn, ready for the egg-and-spoon race, and Jessica was filling the large, sweet jar full of jellybeans, counting carefully under her breath the number she was putting in. The three youths were back under the supervision of Adam, and were recovering the tables, unhitching the foldaway legs that sat hinged underneath. I joined them as they carried the tables into the marquee, and I pointed out just where they needed siting.

Next, the chairs for guests were brought by trolley down the embankment and arranged six to a table under my administration. Circular white linen tablecloths were unpacked and thrown over the wooden structures, hiding the scratched and slightly damaged wooden surfaces.

Just at that very moment the catering van appeared at the top of the drive. I turned to Adam and said, 'Perfect timing; let's get the food unloaded.' We made our way back up the lawn, Adam kicking and pushing and stamping the furrows of earth into ground as we went. The food was all packed into plastic containers and looked delicious: sandwiches of cream cheese with sliced salmon, beef and horse radish, egg and cress and ham salad, rows, and rows of perfect little finger sandwiches. The trays of chocolate eclairs and pastries looked mouthwatering, and I could have eaten two or three there and then.

The caterers carried everything into the marque and prepared the buffet at one end of the tent. A bar had been set up with wine glasses upended on a large silver tray and bottles of red and white wine sitting next to jugs of orange juice.

Suddenly, the music came on really ear-deafeningly and Thomas ran over to turn the volume down. He grinned from ear to ear, which reminded me of Adam. They had the same wide smile, and it felt good to see him enjoying himself.

Just about everything was ready, so I decided to pop up to our apartment and change into my party dress ready to greet anyone who arrived a little early. Adam came to change out of his jeans and sweatshirt and looked very smart in his new chinos and checked shirt. We looked out of the window to the lawned area below us and we both grinned.

'Well, here we go,' Adam said. 'Let's get to the party.'

Guests started to arrive – aunties and uncles whom we had not seen for more than six months, nephews and nieces, grandparents, sisters and their families, lifetime friends and, of course, Phyllis, who arrived in a taxi as she had promised. She looked amazing in her floor-length lilac lacy dress. I really appreciated the fact that at ninety-two years of age she had made all this effort to join us for the afternoon. It being such a sunny warm day she had even brought a matching parasol, which she told me afterwards, her daughter had given to her when she visited the States, to keep off the hot Californian sun. She was quite happy mingling and wandering, chatting to anyone who would lend an ear, amusing strangers with her gossip and sunshine tales of her past life. It was a joy to see her having so much fun. I wished her daughter could have seen her.

We welcomed everyone as they trickled in, and Adam set the party games in motion as soon as everybody had arrived. Thomas oversaw the apple-bobbing and had almost everyone up and round the barrel, when, in turn, most guests tried one way or another to bite into the floating apple or at least get it between their teeth. The timer was on and after several attempts at ducking into the cold water, Grampy Den managed to come up spluttering and gasping with an apple between his teeth. As he smiled, he released the apple and the top set of his dentures fell out and were seen sinking to the bottom of the barrel still contained within the apple.

Thomas was laughing so hard I thought he would split his sides, whilst Grampy Den was most embarrassed and held his hand over the front of his face before dipping his left arm into the icy barrel, trying to locate his upper set. After several minutes of consternation, he plucked them from the barrel and hastily retreated to the lavatory to relocate the false teeth in their rightful place.

Next, everyone was invited to pair up with a partner for the three-legged race. elasticated bands were given out to all competitors and teams were colour-coded into blue, red, green and yellow. The race would start at the marquee and would circumnavigate the Battlefields building, ending up where they had started. There were four teams taking part and each pair was tethered by the ankle. The whistle was blown and off they all went. It was hilarious to see our relatives, the elderly folk and old friends hobbling and strutting into the distance, some tripping as they tried to run faster, while others just could not seem to get synchronised and were kicking each other's ankles as they tried to move in a forward direction.

They all gradually disappeared from view, although they could be heard laughing and cussing from the other side of Battlefields House. Soon enough there appeared from the right of the building a couple who were in their stride and seemed to have no trouble at all in walking two-legged. It was Phyllis and Ben. Phyllis had hitched her lovely long dress into her knickers and her thin stockinged leg was tied resolutely to Ben's thick muscled calf. They were streaking ahead of everyone as they strutted towards the finish line.

Suddenly, close behind came Uncle Leonard and Aunty Val they were well in time with the three-legged race and were catching their competitors coming down the last stretch. Adam was watching next to me and laughing hysterically, picked up the microphone and started commentating as if it was the Grand National.

'And it's neck and neck as the Lilac Lady gallops towards the finish line, followed very closely by Adam's boy. Following at a length and making good ground is Leonard's Buff and Val's-a-Go-Go.'

Phyllis glanced behind and realised they were about to lose the race. She grabbed Ben round the waist and urged him on. Uncle Leonard and Aunty Val could taste victory and were coming up at an ever-increasing rate, but Phyllis and Ben were not going to lose this and put on a sudden spurt. Suddenly, Phyllis's dress unfurled itself from her knickers and tumbled down over her calf to her ankle, it caught in her free foot, and she fell head over heels down the embankment, taking Ben with her. He landed on top of her and, still hitched at the ankle, they rolled down the embankment together, landing at our feet. Only ten yards to go and Phyllis got to her knees, scrambling towards the finish line with Ben in tow. His leg was being stretched beyond its limitations, and he yelped in pain. There was a sudden lunge by Phyllis towards the finish rope and she fell over the line, dragging Ben with her, still tethered at the ankle.

Out of breath and in some discomfort, they sat opposite each other on the grass, still breathing heavily. 'I haven't run like that since my Jack chased me round the bedroom on our twenty-fifth wedding anniversary,' she laughed, gasping for breath.

The race was over and there was only one victorious pair, and that was Phyllis and Ben. I shall never to this day know how they did it, but for a ninety-two-year-old lady, Phyllis certainly had stamina!

It was time for refreshments, and everyone filed into the marquee where Adam had put on some background music. The plates of sandwiches soon emptied, and the glasses filled with alcohol and emptied again and again. Everyone was having a lovely time. Friends sat on the embankment in the sunshine chatting easily, while a merry throng had taken over the dance floor, bopping to an old rendition of 'Tiger Feet' by the once-renowned Mud. The song resonated over the loudspeaker and drew more folk into the marquee until it was overflowing with half-intoxicated, half-euphoric individuals who wanted to just let loose and enjoy the freedom of jiggling their bits and strutting their stuff under the canvas.

Adam found me and suggested we encourage some of the dancers to come out of the marquee as things were a little tight on space. He suggested Ben turn the music off for a few minutes while he tried to organise the egg-and-spoon race. This Ben did, much to the disbelief of the revellers – there were groans from the most inebriated and shouts of, 'I was just getting into that!' and 'Put it back on!'

Adam called everyone to attention and asked for teams of four to be organised for the next race. There was a sudden rush for the tent opening and people spilled out on to the lawn, looking in earnest for the eggs and spoons, eager to participate in the next race. Natural teams were formed, with a few individuals left over, so Adam organised the few remaining green jellies left in the jar and formed the last team of four, so everyone was involved.

Phyllis, I noticed, was in a team with Thomas, Felix and Madalyn. I wondered how she would fare with her long lilac dress this time, as it had caused a catastrophic roll down the embankment earlier. All teams lined up, a few residents a little worse for wear, as the liquor had taken effect over the hot afternoon. Our Cornish friends Chris and Rick were a little unsteady on their feet, but they would be staying with us overnight, along with their teenage children. Thomas was to be evicted from his queen-sized bed and would sleep on the couch; Matt and Rowan would be on the lounge floor in their sleeping bags. It would be a squeeze in Thomas's bed but I felt Chris and Rick would be happy to lay their heads anywhere after a long drive from Cornwall, and a few glasses of red wine

The horn in Adam's hand blasted in my ear, bringing me back

abruptly to the present, and the egg-and-spoon race. The first set of competitors set off at a pace. Aunty Loo was pitted against Aunty Alma, Chris and Cordelia, who was wearing the tightest, short black leather skirt you could imagine. It fitted her rump like two peaches in a silk purse and wobbled as she stepped out in front of the other three competitors. Her high heels had been cast aside and lay on the grass beside a gentleman friend of hers that I had never seen before. He was rather good-looking, tall and casually dressed in tight-fitting jeans, a white open-neck shirt with the sleeves folded, not rolled back, and a gold Rolex wristwatch displayed on a tanned hairy wrist. He must have been ten years younger than Cordelia but that was just my estimation from a distance. It could have been fifteen!

Cordelia was in the lead and reached the end of the lane, where a post marked the turning point. She navigated the post well but as she looked up, the hard-boiled egg wobbled and rolled off the spoon, bouncing on the grass. She bent down quickly, stretching the stitching on her leather covering almost to breaking point, and recovered the egg.

Aunty Loo glanced over as she rounded the pole and was gaining ground. Hot on her heels was Aunty Alma, keeping her hand steady, poised to recover her egg if it should fall. Chris was far behind as she had already dropped her egg several times and had lost too much ground to make up time.

Aunty Loo had taken the lead and was heading down the long stretch to the finishing line, her family members were shouting out and urging her on, and she was giggling as she came down the last few yards and ran over the red tape to cheers from her two sons.

Cordelia was looking flustered and held on to her spoon

tightly as she followed, Aunty Alma was next to finish to whoops and applause from Uncle Trevor, Warren and Ian, her two sons. Chris had dropped her egg yet again and came in last,

The next four stepped up: God-daughter Stephanie, nephew Christopher, Uncle Leonard and Helen from number one.

The horn went again and off they trotted. Adam picked up the microphone connected to the loudspeaker system again and started a running commentary on the race.

'All the way from Brisbane, Australia, and fresh off a Boeing seven-eight-seven Dreamliner, is Stephanie, a fine filly! Wearing the colours of the Australian flag, she has taken the lead. Coming a close second is Helen, steady as she goes; Helen is wearing the number one from her apartment on her back, looking confident as she strides into second place behind the striking figure of Stephanie. Cousin Christopher, the elder of the siblings, a strong handsome contender is making ground as he gets into his stride, gaining on the field of runners. But there has been a fall at the post – Uncle Leonard has taken a tumble at the turn; he's down, egg lying crushed beneath him. Is he going to finish the race? It's looking doubtful! But he is up and he's recovered his legs. Yes! He is back up and the egg, although crushed, is back on the spoon. Now limping along and obviously in some discomfort. Let's hope, ladies and gentlemen of the Battlefields party, that he will not have to be put down because of his injury There was a roar from the gathered spectators as Uncle Leonard hobbled down the last straight. Folk were clapping and urging him on.

Adam was in full flow as he commentated on the race, thoroughly enjoying his time at the microphone.

'It's four to one odds on Stephanie who wins the second race at the Battlefields racecourse this afternoon. Congratulations to the winner by a length – it's Stephanie!' A roar went up from the spectators and Stephanie held her hand high in recognition of the feat she had just accomplished. She commented later that it was worth the flight from Australia just to win the egg-and-spoon race!

Minutes later the next four contestants lined up and Adam continued the commentary and introduced the field.

'Uncle Steve, the fine gelding all the way from the Whitchurch Stables near Bristol; a grey with pedigree, wearing the red-and-white colours of his home team Bristol City. A long history of placements in the Irish sweepstakes over the past three years and the favourite in this race at four to one. Alongside Uncle Steve, saddled up and rearing to go, is Uncle Trevor, stabled together at the Badminton Estate and training alongside each other this past year. A very good jumper, I'm told, clearing the four foot ten inches high fence at Becher's Brook at Aintree last year and coming a close third. A little heavy round the girth but worth a punt.'

This commentary carried on throughout the next four races, until almost everyone had competed in a length of the lawn. It was hilarious to watch, but everyone seemed to enjoy the race.

Ben reminded me about the enlarged, framed Battlefields drone photograph and we hastened to recover it from the basement before people had a chance to leave the party. As yet I hadn't had the time to unwrap the print from the large brown sheets it had been carefully wrapped in. So, I was keen and excited to see the result of our super-enlarged print.

We presented it to Adam in front of all the guests, who had

been summoned to the embankment. He unwrapped it, tearing the brown paper and pulling off the string to reveal a large, framed photograph of Battlefields from above. He was delighted with it, congratulating us on a wonderful gift that he said he would treasure forever.

It was not until later when we were in our apartment and Adam had hung the photograph on the wall, that Chris, being a keen photographer and admiring the picture closely, remarked on the fact that no one had noticed the two figures on the roof, sunbathing in the nude!

'What!' a stunned Adam had said, as we all crowded in to have a better look.

Ben retrieved the magnifying glass from the drawer and scrutinised the photograph. 'Oh my God,' he said in a half-amused, shocked voice. 'It's Helen and Michael!'

I burst out laughing and said, 'It was that hot sunny day a few weeks ago when Philip called to do the aerial-photography; I never got round to telling Helen and Michael that the drone would be flying over for several minutes later that afternoon. They must have been asleep on the roof at the time.'

'Well,' Adam said, 'we had better keep this to ourselves because if it got out, we might be fined or taken to court for infringement of human rights.'

Back at the party there were more drinks, and the individuals that could summon up the strength to boogie were still dancing, while a few folks were saying their goodbyes. Dusk was starting to fall and as friends and family made their way home, we cleared away the food and tidy the lawn area of chairs and tables.

The marquee company were coming the following morning

to remove the tent, chairs, tables and all the trimmings, and this time they would be carrying the tables up to the carpark and not rolling them down the hill! The aerial photograph stayed on the wall and raised many an eyebrow when friends visited, but, whenever we had a management meeting in our apartment, it was taken down and hidden away from prying eyes. Just in case!

CHAPTER 19

THE DETECTORIST

The following year early in February the Battlefields management committee had a written request from a local historian who was researching the Battle of Lansdowne, a site nearby where the first English Civil War had taken place. He wished to invite a few of us to meet up with him to discuss the battle and was keen to pass on his historical knowledge to anyone that might be interested.

I thought it would be fascinating, and my curiosity was aroused along with Jeremy and Jessica's. We arranged to meet the following Monday on the lawn, and Theodore Gough-Claythorpe introduced himself as not only a local historian but a detectorist. Now, as we were unsure of what exactly a detectorist did, we let him talk without interruption.

Eventually, after a long-winded explanation and an even lengthier account of the battle that took place in 1643, he proceeded to ask permission to bring along his metal detector and spend a weekend covering the lawn and wooded area surrounding our Gothic residence. We were on board immediately and eagerly questioned him about the battle.

It transpired that on 5 July in the year 1643, the armies of Sir

Ralph Hopton and William Waller were at war. The two opposing armies, Hopton being the head of the Royalist army and Waller in charge of Parliament's troops, were engaging in battle along the steep slopes of Lansdown. Despite repeated cavalry charges by the Parliamentarian army and the loss of men and horses, Waller was forced to retire behind a high dry-stone wall at the top of a hill in Lansdowne where combat ensued through the night. Neither army was willing to submit or move from cover.

But later that night under the cover of darkness it was the Parliamentarians who abandoned their position, leaving lanterns atop the walls to outsmart their enemies, who mistakenly believed that their position was held.

It was all very interesting and we agreed to let Theodore proceed with the search, on condition that there were no objections from the management committee. The call went round, and it was viewed by everyone that Theodore Gough-Claythorpe should be allowed to proceed with his quest.

It was noted in the committee records later that Francesco proposed, if any excavations around Battlefields were disturbed there should be a clause to restore the earth back to its original state and in the event of any discoveries, the treasures found would be shared among Theodore and the residents.

After Francesco's ranting were quelled, it was agreed that Theodore would commence the following weekend.

He arrived that Saturday morning in his large four- he drove down the driveway and parked up in front of the house. He looked like the squire in *To the Manor Born* with his tweed jacket, green Hunter wellington boots and long weatherproof Brontë full-length wax cotton coat.

Jessica and Jeremy were with me to greet our new detectorist. His handshake was strong and very vigorous as he clasped each of our hands in turn. After the initial greeting we walked with Theodore down the embankment towards the edge of the wood, where the pungent smell of wild garlic filled our nostrils.

'I'll start at the edge of the wood and sweep in a northerly direction,' he said as he glanced at a small compass in his hand. 'No need for you to stay,' he said. 'I'll find you if I need you.'

I volunteered to bring him a cup of coffee at ten o'clock and left him sorting out his metal detector and headphones as we walked back up the bank. I glanced over my shoulder as I reached the edge of the car park and he was in full sweep mode, swinging the metal detector in a wide arc, covering as much ground as his arms allowed. I wondered if he would uncover a treasure trove of gold trinkets or a hoard of Roman coins. I said farewell to Jeremy and Jessica and made my way back up to the apartment.

At ten a.m. true to my word, I took a small tray of coffee and biscuits down to find Theodore. He was facing away from me and obviously transfixed with his business. I found him unaware of my presence, so I touched him on the shoulder, causing him to wheel round suddenly, catching my ankle with his metal detector.

It caught me right on the anklebone, causing me to let out a shriek. I dropped the tray, spilling the coffee all down my jeans, scalding my skin as it seeped through the fabric. The biscuits fell to the grass, along with the tray, sugar bowl and milk jug.

'So sorry,' Theodore spluttered. He took off his earphones and laid the metal detector on the grass while he continued to apologise profusely.

'It really wasn't your fault,' I said, dabbing at the large wet patch across my jeans. 'I'm sorry if I startled you – I can get you another coffee if you would like one.' He agreed that another coffee was a good idea and asked if I was all right and not too badly burned, and if my ankle was damaged.

Feeling a little embarrassed, I assured him that no harm had been done. But under the wet fabric I felt a red burning feeling where the hot liquid had penetrated and scalded my skin. I retreated to the apartment, trying not to limp under the pain inflicted by the metal detector to my ankle. I hastily replaced my wet clothes and checked the skin on my ankle, which had a deep cut. A red patch had appeared on the top of my thigh, luckily, it wasn't a scald as the coffee had been in the cafetière a good five minutes before it had done any real damage, but a painful wound had been inflicted on my foot as well, which still stung.

The kettle boiled once again, I replaced everything on the tray – biscuits, new coffee cups and a cafetière of freshly brewed coffee – and hobbled back down the stairs to our detectorist. This time I made sure to attract Theodore's attention first without getting too close!

He was grateful for the coffee and, putting his metal detector aside, stopped for a chat. He told me he had been metal-detecting for about fifteen years and had a degree in archaeology. He had become interested in the Battle of Lansdowne when he moved into the area a year ago. He now lived near Bath and was involved with the Holburne Museum, curating exhibitions.

He told me of a rare find he had made when detecting in Salisbury. He, along with another detectorist, had uncovered a hoard of Roman coins that were more than 1,700 years old.

They had uncovered coins dating back to as early as AD 253 when Valerian I had ruled the empire. The earthenware pot had contained 200 coins of significant interest and value. They now resided in the British Museum. It all sounded very exciting and interesting.

Well time was of the essence, and Theodore wanted to continue with his sweeping, so I left him to it.

It was not until late in the afternoon that the apartment door intercom buzzed. It was Theodore and he was excited to pass on the knowledge that he had a confirmation of a dull beep from his detecting instrument on the lawn. I popped on my jacket and limped down the stairway to open the front door, where Theodore was waiting for me. Jeremy and Jessica were already on the lawn, hovering in anticipation.

As we walked across to the site of interest, which now had been marked with white spray in a large rectangle shape, Theodore asked our permission to make an incision in the grass and dig down a few feet to see if he could uncover anything of interest. We readily agreed and offered our help, but Theodore was insistent that he needed to proceed cautiously so as not to damage the site.

He worked carefully round the rectangle, digging meticulously with his spade and carefully removing, shovel by shovel, the soil from the grass; he piled the turf beside the ever-increasing hole in the lawn. After replacing his earphones and sweeping the area yet again to try and detect the item that was creating the buzzing noise on his metal detector, he became very excited! 'There is something down there,' he said, smiling.

A couple of residents came out of the building to see what

was going on. Felix and Madalyn, Felicity and Daniel and Helen and Michael all eventually joined the group. There was exuberant chatter amongst all the residents as to what it might be under the ground.

Twenty minutes went by and still nothing was found. Cordelia eventually came along with a deckchair under one arm; her other hand was holding a cocktail glass containing a green liquid. She enquired as to what was going on and Felix took it upon himself to enlighten her about the unfolding situation.

Jeremy went off to find a bottle of wine and some glasses, saying that it could be a long night. Helen and Michael disappeared and then returned with two kitchen chairs and a bottle of *Pinot Grigio* and a plate of cheese straws, which they passed around to the growing group.

The last to join the merry throng were Francesco and Lena, who wandered over to the group. The first thing Francesco said was, 'What a bloody mess; how deep is he going?' and 'I hope he's going to fill in the hole after he's finished his dig to Australia.' As usual, this sort of cynical comment did not help!

A large group now stood or sat around the excavation, drinking and eating the few offerings of biscuits and crisps that were being passed around. The light was fading and even though the moon had come up, Theodore was still digging in the soil. His head was now well below the level of the lawn and still bucketloads of soil were being handed up and tipped out creating a large muddy mound. Francesco was getting increasingly worried about the size and depth of the excavation, and there were a few grumblings from other residents too.

Finally, Theodore peeped over the rim and said he would call it a night. He climbed out of the hole with great difficulty, Felix giving him his hand and pulling him roughly on to the lawn. He said that he would return at first light and finish the dig. Whatever was down there Theodore would recover it tomorrow morning.

Francesco stepped forward and stood in front of a very weary, mud-streaked Theodore and said, 'You can't leave it there!' Theodore became a little flustered and apologised for the mess but felt that as it was getting dark, it might not be wise to carry on digging.

'Rubbish,' said Francesco. 'Finish off the dig – it will take you all day tomorrow to fill this bloody great hole in.'

Several residents, now feeling the effects of many bottles of wine and most of them enjoying the quiet but exciting evening, were egging Theodore on too.

'Very well then, if you want me to excavate further then you will have to help me.'

Felix rolled up his sleeves and jumped down into the large grave-like hole. 'Throw me down the spade!' he shouted. 'Let's see what's down here.'

It took several attempts by willing residents to shift another foot of soil; by then the earthen mountain was piled high and spreading out across the finely manicured lawn.

Theodore requested another sweep with the metal detector before a final hover and a yelp! He scraped something hard with his spade. 'It's here! I can feel something hard.'

We all gathered round and peered into the hole in the ground. Jeremy shone a torch and picked out Theodore's spade as it hit the object. Jessica shone her mobile on to the spot where

Theodore was scraping at the article. Francesco got down on his knees as if in prayer and leaned over the hole.

With great difficulty Theodore scraped with his hands in the earth to reveal the hidden treasure. He held it up into the torchlight and in a slightly decorous voice, announced it was a cannon ball. There was a stunned silence all around! It was as if the world had stopped spinning.

Francesco let out a loud 'Nooooo, I don't believe it!' before pulling himself on to his feet with Lena's help and storming off in the direction of his apartment and a hot bath, to ease his aching heart and arthritic knee.

Theodore stood holding the muddy, rusting cannon ball in the torchlight. It was a seventeenth-century English Civil War cannon ball, made of iron and measuring a grand sixty-one millimetres, according to Theodore's tape measure. It had probably been used at the Battle of Lansdowne, explained Theodore, feeling quite pleased with himself. He had at least found a relic of the Civil War.

But no one was interested and just about everyone turned and wandered back to their apartments, carrying their chairs and empty bottles, with mutterings of disappointment and resignation. It was left to me, Adam, Jessica and Jeremy to congratulate Theodore on his magnificent find.

'Is it worth anything?' asked Adam, hoping that at least it might be something an antique collector might like.

'To be honest,' said the detectorist, 'it might fetch seventy to eighty pounds on eBay, if you are lucky.'

'Well, that's something,' I said, trying to lighten the mood.

'You can have it, if you want it,' offered Theodore. I gratefully accepted the muddy gift, and Adam took the heavy object and shook hands with Theodore. 'I will come back tomorrow and fill in the hole,' he said a little sheepishly.

'Good man,' said Adam. 'We will help you.'

We carried the dirty ball of iron back to our apartment and put it into the washing-up bowl, leaving it overnight to soak and to hopefully reveal at least something of interest in the morning. We went to bed that night feeling very light-headed after the copious amounts of wine we had drunk, and rather amused at the ridiculous amount of time we had spent at the dig, wondering if we had uncovered a treasure trove of gigantic proportions in the gardens of Battlefields.

As promised Theodore returned the following morning and with our help refilled the large gaping rectangle that had been excavated the day before. No one ever asked after the cannon ball, so we eventually wrapped it up in a piece of newspaper and a rag and deposited it in the cellar for future residents to ponder over.

CHAPTER 20

DECISIONS! DECISIONS!

It was on a Tuesday evening when Adam, having finished work, came through the front door, and what he said threw all my thoughts and plans into turmoil.

'I've got some news,' he said with a serious look on his face. I waited to hear what this news could possibly be. Was he being given a raise? Had he decided he wanted to buy a dog? Had he won a million on the Premium Bonds?

He went on to say that he had had a long conversation with Al his American boss who worked on the other side of the Atlantic and ran the large American corporation in Los Angeles. I waited unsure of what he was about to tell me… what was he was going to say?

'It's like this,' he said continuing the one-sided conversation and watching me closely to gauge my reaction as to what he was about relay. 'He's offering me a position – it's running one of the underperforming companies for the corporation. Problem is . . . it's in L.A.'

I uttered an expletive! Then gathering my thoughts, which were rushing like wildfire through my brain, I asked, 'Is that what you want? Is it a permanent position in the States; where would we live? What about Thomas and Ben? Would they be able to go to L.A.?'

'Hold on,' said Adam. 'Nothing's been settled; I told Al I would have to talk it over with you and the family as it was a joint decision and there was a lot to think about.' Adam went on, 'Al has asked that before we decide anything he would like us to go over to Los Angeles for a week, all expenses paid.' Adam could meet the team that he would be responsible for, see the head offices and get a feeling for the job and all that it had to offer.

I had accompanied Adam several times over the six years he had been working for the corporation when on many occasions he had been called over to give an annual business presentation. Al had been generous in allowing me to accompany Adam on the trips if we paid for the flight cost for myself. I was welcome to stay at the hotel with Adam and as always, we tagged on a family holiday at our own expense, after Adam had finished his business with the company.

This had given us the opportunity to visit California, including San Francisco and the pacific coastal region. many times, and we had enjoyed it immensely, but living there permanently was another 'ball game'.

Adam went on to say, 'Let's keep open minds; let's take the opportunity to at least travel to L.A., all expenses paid. I'm happy to go over and talk things through with Al – I've always got on well with him and he obviously thinks I'm the right man for the job, otherwise he wouldn't have offered the position to me.'

I wondered if Adam was secretly hoping that we might consider seriously the chance of a new life and only needed my go-ahead to set us on a path that would change the direction of our lives forever.

'Look, nothing is set in Californian concrete,' he said with a mischievous smile. 'Why don't we take this golden opportunity of an all-expenses-paid vacation in sunny Los Angeles for a week. I think we should at least find out more detail. I will meet up with Al, get the lay of the land, see what package he is offering and take it from there. He has offered us return tickets on an Air New Zealand flight, business class, five-star accommodation in a fantastic hotel in Santa Monica and all expenses paid while we are visiting California. At the end of the week if you are dead against the idea, then you will have the last word.'

He smiled and came over and gave me a hug. 'It will be OK, I promise.'

Adam was obviously really excited about the offer, and I owed him this much. I was feeling excited about the vacation but the prospect of upping sticks, leaving Battlefields and moving across the pond was terrifying!

Adam offered to make a cup of tea while I got used to the idea and I wandered over to the large casement window and looked out at the surrounding trees. The leafy branches seemed to be waving at me in the wind. The clouds on the horizon were dark and moody and I knew rain was heading our way very soon. Maybe sunny California might not be a bad thing for a week, just to help me decide one way or the other.

I knew that if Ben and Thomas were against the idea then there was no chance of us going, as we would not be going without them.

When we told Ben about the job offer later that night and

the chance of a free week's holiday for Adam and me, we were surprised at his response. He was very positive and encouraging and insisted we go for the week and keep an open mind. He had few reservations about leaving Battlefields and was only concerned that we would wait until the end of the year until he had finished his degree.

Thomas was surprised when we told him but one of those big McKenzie grins spread across his face, and he let out a 'Wow! Didn't see that coming!' He enquired as to whether we were thinking of inviting him along and we assured him we would not go without him if we did decide to leave the UK. Even though he was settled in his own place, he had no real ties, no serious girlfriend, a job that could be transferred to the US, if necessary, and a great sense of adventure, so that was a great relief. It was only us we had to satisfy, then.

This positive energy carried us through until July. After many long conversations with Al on Zoom and lots of reassurance from family and friends, we agreed we would go over to California on the fourth of September, the day after Adam's birthday.

During the following month we received travel documents, air-flight times and information on our five-star hotel accommodation in L.A. We were staying in the Marina Hotel right on Marina Del Ray harbourside. The flight was from Heathrow Airport at 11.05 a.m., and we were flying with Air New Zealand.

We told the residents at Battlefields about our trip but kept the real reason for our departure to ourselves for the time being. Adam said there was no need to throw everybody into confusion over the fact that the McKenzie's' might be immigrating and number three might be up for sale soon and we may leave Battlefields forever. That would happen all in good time, *if* . . . that was our decision on our return.

The journey to California finally arrived after what seemed like an eternity. The cases were packed, our flight information, plans for the week and tickets were safely in Adam's travel pouch, and it was really happening.

Ben had got up especially early to wave us off from the turret window, still in his pyjamas. Giving him an enormous hug and ruffling his untidy hair I told him we would keep in touch via text and email and send lots of pictures of California, the beaches and area where we might live. He kissed me on the cheek and punched Adam on the shoulder wishing us well on our adventure. Adam picked up the cases and we headed down the cantilever stairway and out into the carpark. The suitcases were loaded into the boot of the Range Rover, and we jumped in. I looked up from the car as we made our way along the winding drive away from Battlefields and Bens little figure in the apartment window. I waved as he went out of sight. I wished the boys were coming with us on our week's adventure, but the all-expenses-paid trip did not include Ben and Thomas.

CHAPTER 21

ACROSS THE POND

When we arrived at Heathrow Airport, we left the car in the long-stay parking area and caught the transfer bus to Terminal 5. As soon as we entered the sliding doors at the Air New Zealand check-in desk, we were ushered through as priority guests by a lovely lady, who was obviously expecting us as we were greeted with 'Welcome to Air New Zealand, Mr and Mrs McKenzie If you would like to follow me, I will check you both in.'

I glanced over to Adam, and he winked and smiled as if to say. *Not bad.* Our luggage was taken from us by a very smart airline employee in a light blue suit sporting a smart NZ airline emblem in gold. Luggage labels were attached and then loaded on to a waiting trolley, which then disappeared through two sliding doors.

'This is what business class is all about,' Adam whispered in my ear.

'I could get used to this!' I laughed.

We were taken through security, where there was a short queue, and then on directed to the lounge where reserved comfortable reclining leather chairs waited for us. The gentleman concierge offered to show me around the amenities, pointing out the salad bar, hot soups, a wide array of cooked meals available at our request, hot bread rolls to accompany the delicious-looking turkey soup, and a tea and coffee machine that looked state-of-the-art as well as wine, spirits and liquors to drink at our leisure. It was a real treat to be here enjoying all the luxuries that there were on offer and Adam and I soaked it all up.

We kept in touch via WhatsApp with Ben and Thomas throughout our time at the airport and they were very excited to hear all about it.

After a couple of hours relaxing in the lounge, Adam checked the gate number and boarding time. He came over and said our flight had been called and it was time to leave the luxuries of the lounge for stage two of our journey.

On boarding the aeroplane, we were shown to our seats in business class, which looked like a set from a Hollywood movie. The cabin was a step up from our usual flight on EasyJet from Bristol International. On finding our seat numbers, we were treated to strawberry shortcake and a champagne flute of Bollinger served on a little silver tray.

Adam was sitting opposite me in his large reclining seat. He pulled out a folded flat screen from its station and proceeded to take earphones from a side pocket. These were tied up in a little black pouch with drawstrings with the NZ logo printed on the front, the same logo I had seen on the baggage-handler's lapel earlier.

Adam pointed to the side pocket of the seat, so I looked for mine and found them. After finding the earphone access point, I plugged them in. Adam leant across the aisle and showed me how to access all the different programmes available for the flight – TV, radio and films. I settled back, sipping my champagne, and selected *La La Land*, a film I had missed when it was out at the cinema the year previously.

Just as I was getting into the story, a young flight attendant pulled back the cabin curtain that separated the crew from the passengers and came over. He bent down to eye level and smiled graciously. He introduced himself as Michael, pointing to his lapel on his tight- fitting waistcoat where a gold italic name badge was pinned.

'I am here to look after you both whilst on our flight in any way I can,' he said. 'If there is anything you require – drinks, hot beverages, wines, spirits, snacks or advice – please press this button on your screen and I'll pop along.' He smiled again as he stood up and I smelt a waft of eau de cologne as he returned to the crew's quarters.

Just at that moment the captain's voice came over the intercom telling us the flight details and how he would keep us up to date on our journey with information on our progress. He also mentioned the fact that we were leaving the rain in England for the sunshine of California. It would be an eleven-hour flight, and he hoped we would enjoy the journey with Air New Zealand. *Ping-Pong!*

I glanced out of the aircraft window where rain dribbled down the pane. I was not sorry to be leaving the English weather behind, but I was missing Ben and Thomas already. They had been very excited for us and our trip and seemed quite enthusiastic about the possibility of emigrating as a family, but I still had so many reservations. Well, perhaps I might be persuaded one way or another after our trip. *Who knows?* I thought to myself.

The flight took off on time and we gently rose into the air like a gigantic bird drifting through the misty rainclouds where visibility was dark and foggy. Suddenly, we were above the grey haze, and the brightness of the sun shone through the cabin window. The rain on the window ran at right angles on the glass, as we flew at speed, and ran in rivulets across the porthole before drying to reveal a bank of cloud below us.

I looked down at the cotton-wool scene below. I had always enjoyed flying above the clouds. It was a magical bird's-eye view, and it amazed me to see just how beautiful our planet was from the air. This trip was going to be amazing!

I settled back into the comfortable chair when Adam unbuckled his seat belt and came across the aisle. He bent down next to me and whispered in my ear. 'Don't look now but I think that's Robbie Williams over there!' I craned my neck and looked over Adam's shoulder to where he was discreetly pointing his finger, trying to see if he had spotted a look-alike or to see if he was indeed joking, but to my surprise, Robbie Williams was sitting in a booth the other side of Adam's aisle with his earphones on, watching a film. He was sitting on his own and his wife, Ayda, was directly in front of him occupying the forward booth.

'It is!' I whispered. 'It is really Robbie Williams! He must be flying to his Los Angeles home for the winter.' I had read on the internet that he had a villa up in the Californian mountains somewhere, and I had been a Take That fan for as long as I could remember. 'Wow, the boys will never believe me about this!' I gushed.

A couple of other passengers had noticed the celebrity accompanying us on the plane and were discreetly glancing in Robbie's direction, but nobody rushed over to ask for his autograph or even acknowledged his presence. I guess everyone deserves their privacy and I could imagine Ayda would not be too happy if numerous fans of Robbie were badgering him while he was enjoying a quiet flight back home. I must admit that I did take a few extra visits to the ladies the long way round the plane so I could get an extra glance in his direction.

Our personal attendant appeared from behind the dark blue partition curtain once again and came towards Adam and me. In his left hand he held a small silver tray on which a little box rested. In his right hand he held a large pair of silver tweezers. I wondered what he was going to say or do with the tweezers.

'Would you like a warm, moist –' *Wherever was he going with this?* – 'hand towel to wipe your hands before we serve lunch?' He smiled down at me.

I breathed a sigh of relief and uttered, 'Oh yes, please, that would be nice.'

He picked up the small towel with the overly large silver tweezers and dropped it into my cupped hands. It was warm and moist, as described by Michael, and I wiped my hands on the cloth and passed it back to him. He pinched the soiled flannel expertly between the tweezers and popped it on the tray, then promptly returned to the crew's quarters before returning to Adam with a fresh towel.

It was a joy to watch this man in motion. I wondered how many times he had dished out warm, damp towels and how many celebrity hands his little cloths had cleansed.

Moments later, back Michael came, this time with dinner menus for us to peruse at our leisure. The choice was overwhelming.

Appetiser

* Fritters of potatoes and Jerusalem artichokes with Gorgonzola
* Rolled chicken with sweet Gorgonzola and pomegranate

Starter

* Duck breast with orange star anise gastrique, fungus and ginger sesame slaw
* Char siu pork, green beans with Chinese olive preserve, black mushrooms, pickled yellow radish and hoisin mayonnaise

From the bakery

* Pumpkin and polenta loaf, purple grain rolls and garlic bread offered with Hawke's Bay extra virgin olive oil.

Mains

* Beef fillet with kūmara and red onions cooked in balsamic, horseradish and beetroot chrain
* Chermoula-rubbed salmon with spiced cauliflower and cardamom couscous, rocket salad
* Spicy Korean chicken with pickled white radish, steamed rice and sesame and chilli vegetables

To finish

* Pistachio mousse with lemon-infused rosewater glaze and strawberry gel

* Dark chocolate and hazelnut praline *delice*
* Fresh fruit plate

As if this mouthwatering selection was not enough to tempt me, there was a note to help yourself to snacks available throughout the flight.

As well as the limitless supply of cocktails, wines and spirits and the occasional cup of tea, I was beginning to think they should be charging us for the extra weight we would be putting on during the flight!

I made my choices, and Michael presently came and took down my order, congratulating me on choosing the salmon, which he highly recommended. The pop-out tray was popped out by Michael and the TV screen pushed a little further back to accommodate the food now being offered and dished on to a New Zealand gold-rimmed plate.

The food was as good as it looked and I ate every morsel, followed by the dark chocolate hazelnut and praline *delice*, something that tasted as near heaven as it could have possibly been!

A glass of cold cranberry juice with ice in the shape of little aircraft was about all I could manage to wash the tasty meal down.

I settled back and waited for Michael to appear, which happened almost instantly. He asked if I had enjoyed the meal and after assuring him that it had all been delicious, he swept the dirty crockery and napkin away in a flourish and disappeared back behind the curtain once again.

Adam gave me a grin and leant across and asked if I was enjoying all the attention I was receiving, and I nodded. 'This is amazing!' I replied laughing.

'Just you wait. We have only just started.' Adam winked.

We settled back once again into our reclining seats and spent the next two hours enjoying films on the screen, earphones on and in our own little worlds. I glanced across at Adam several times and he was dozing with a contented look on his face. This was a big chance for him in a large American corporation. Al obviously thought very highly of him and was giving him this once-in-a-lifetime opportunity.

If Adam thought the right decision was to go with the offer on the table, then would I be brave enough to take this opportunity and agree we should go. I had asked myself that question so many times in the past few weeks and I really could not come to a decision.

For now, I was happy to go along on this adventure, explore all the possibilities on offer and together we would sink or swim! After all, if Al had every confidence in Adam's ability to step up, then I should have the confidence and positivity to say *Let's do it!*

My film came to an end and, even though I had been in deep thought while watching it, I was feeling positive about the whole situation.

Michael reappeared with beverages and snacks and, while thirty thousand feet high, flying across the Atlantic Ocean, I sat back to enjoy my English breakfast cup of tea and shortbread biscuits.

Time for another film and a chat to Adam across the aisle. I strained my neck once again to see past my husband, only to find Robbie cuddled up under an Air New Zealand blanket, eye mask on and oblivious to the occasional flight passenger meandering to the toilets.

Michael came back to remove cups and saucers and offered to show me how to turn my upholstered chair conveniently into a remarkably comfortable bed. With a flick of a switch the chair slid backwards, and a footrest appeared from below. Michael produced a small white cotton pillow and, to my delight, a matching New Zealand blanket identical to the one that I had seen covering Robbie earlier.

Adam suggested I get a few hours' sleep before we arrived at Los Angeles, so I snuggled down. Even though the seat belt was still clipped in place should there be any turbulence, I was very comfortable and fell asleep dreaming of the Californian beaches and the blue ocean beneath us.

Several hours later I was woken by the dimmed lighting brightening and . . . *PING-PONG*! The captain's voice came over the tannoy system announcing the weather situation in California. He told us the weather forecast for the coming week was bright sunshine and a balmy twenty-three degrees Celsius, which I calculated to be about seventy-six degrees Fahrenheit. Very comfortable!

Our friendly air steward Michael came over carrying a hot-towel tray and once again I accepted the moist white square, wiping my face and neck and banishing the sleep from my eyes.

Adam leant across and squeezed my hand. 'You slept like a log,' he said. 'Must be all those travel sickness pills you took.' He was probably right. I always suffered with motion sickness and relied on my travel sickness tablets to get me from A to B when flying.

I returned my convenient bed back into a chair and stored the pillow and blanket under the seat and sat up.

Adam asked if I wanted to stretch my legs and suggested we went out into the galley, which we did. Sarah, another flight attendant, looked across and offered snacks – crisps, chocolate bars and mints – but we politely declined and explained that we had only come out to stretch our muscles and do a few exercises.

'Please feel free,' she said with a smile. 'You might like to look out of the cabin-door window,' she volunteered. 'We are just passing over Greenland.'

I looked out and down through the porthole window and could see an expanse of dark blue ocean, littered with tiny broken fragments of white irregular shapes and sizes like a shattered mirror. They stretched as far as my eye could see and dotted the ocean. They were icebergs, thousands of them just floating across the dark blue expanse.

Adam came over and we watched from above and we both thought it was a magical experience. Sarah had taken the time to point this phenomenon out to us. She told us she always looked out for it as she flew this route many times and she never failed to be amazed at the views from the aircraft at such a height. It was a very special moment as we peered down at the earth together.

The rest of the flight passed by quickly and after a hearty breakfast with orange juice and more cups of English breakfast tea, the announcement finally came that we would be landing in approximately twenty minutes.

The landing was as smooth as you would expect from an experienced Air New Zealand pilot, and we finally taxied to a standstill. I could not help glancing over at the Williams celebrity and then suddenly, Ayda got up and was heading towards the pulled curtain that separated the two classes, leaving Robbie on his own.

Adam looked over and said, 'Why don't you ask him for his autograph?'

'What?' I said.

'Ask him for his autograph,' he suggested.

I told him I did not have anything to write on and Adam handed me a napkin and a pen. 'It will be your only chance to get his autograph.' He grinned at me.

'Right,' I said. I did not waste a minute. If I had stopped to think about what I was about to do I would have chickened out . . . but this would be my only ever chance to get his autograph, Ayda would be back any second, they would be off the plane and that would be that! Opportunity gone!

I took the napkin and the Air New Zealand pen and marched round the cabin confidently until I came to the seat Robbie had just arisen from. He had his back to me and was just about to open the luggage overhead locker when I tapped him on the shoulder.

'Excuse me, Robbie,' I said like a starstruck ten-year-old, 'but do you think I could have your autograph?' He turned round to look at me and smiled, and I think I must have turned a dark shade of beetroot.

'Sure,' he said. 'Who should I make it out to?'

I asked him to make it out to me and he asked my name. I told him and he signed his name with love. I told him my two sons would never believe me if I had not had him sign the napkin and he smiled and said, 'No problem.'

I thanked him and returned to my seat before Ayda returned and ushered him out of the aircraft, surrounded by three security guys dressed in black who had mysteriously appeared from nowhere.

I saw the back of Robbie as he disappeared down the aircraft stairs, quickly followed by his entourage. I looked at Adam, who was grinning widely. I don't think he could believe what I had just done.

The napkin and the pen were stowed away for posterity in my hand luggage, and I followed Adam out of the aircraft, thanking the flight attendants as we floated down from cloud nine.

Passengers filed out of the aircraft, all going off to other destinations, some reboarding in a couple of hours to complete their journey to New Zealand, another long journey. Adam and I followed a group of people to passport control, where we spotted Robbie and Ayda heading off in another direction, through another exit reserved for celebrity and important passengers. I got my camera out to take a quick snap, but a large American security guard came running my way.

'Ma'am! No photographs in passport control.' He looked very serious and had a holster with a gun clipped in it. I apologised and Adam quickly took over the awkward situation.

'My wife is a fan; it's Robbie Williams you see just over there.' Adam pointed in the direction of a couple disappearing through double doors surrounded by the same guys dressed in black.

'No photography,' he repeated without smiling! 'Continue to passport control this way.' He pointed to the desk where passengers were now queuing. I quickly pushed my camera back into its bag and followed Adam.

'Welcome to America,' a passenger passing by said, who had witnessed our little episode.

Adam produced our passports, and we were taken fast track ahead of the queue, where a travel control officer, dressed in black shirt, black tie and trousers, looked us up and down. Adam handed over personal documents and waited

'Are you on business or pleasure?' he asked as he looked Adam straight in the eye.

'A bit of both,' Adam laughed lightly.

The security guy did not raise a smile or acknowledge the light-hearted reply. 'Where will you be staying?' he asked.

Adam explained that we were staying in the Marina Del Ray Hotel for five days. The officer passed back the passports and folded our documentation and with a dark skinny hand waved us through the immigration aisle. 'Have a good day,' he muttered as we passed through.

We entered a large room and were told to take a seat as our luggage would be with us shortly. Apparently, it would be collected from the luggage return and brought out for us. I was liking this business-class attention!

Within ten minutes along came the luggage, transported on a large trolley, pushed by an immaculately dressed concierge. Adam fumbled in his pocket for some American coins and tipped the guy. The concierge touched his cap and disappeared with the empty trolley, leaving our cases on the floor next to us.

An empty baggage trolley was parked nearby so Adam walked across and brought it over, loading our large cases and hand luggage on to it. 'This way, ma'am,' Adam said in an American accent. The sliding doors opened automatically, and we headed out of the airport.

CHAPTER 22

CALIFORNIAN SUNSHINE

The heat of the Californian sunshine hit us like the hot blast from an oven door when you open it midway through cooking an apple pie! The bright light of the sun contrasted with the airport terminal. I followed Adam as he pushed the heavy trolley on to the pavement.

'I'll flag down a taxi,' he said as he walked to the edge of the road, looking up and down, not sure which one to choose as they were everywhere, like bees round a honey pot.

It did not take him long before one of the famous yellow taxi cabs pulled up with a little screech. A happy chappie with a big cheeky grin alighted and popped open his trunk (*boot* to us in the UK, not the swimming kind!) and started loading our cases in the back. He picked them up like they were full of feathers and stacked them neatly in the trunk.

He opened the rear door of the taxi for us to climb in and jumped into the front seat, glancing back at us, and enquired very respectfully, 'Where to, sir?'

As I settled into my seat, Adam gave the address of the hotel we were staying in then sat back and breathed a sigh of relief.

'Chapter one complete!' he said.

He had always, from the first time I had met him, divided his day, week, or year into chapters, turning the page on a completed day or mission like he was completing a book. The irony of this was where was his book taking us? Would this be our final chapter? Moving to the US – was this the story we would tell our grandchildren and great-grandchildren? If we ever had any! It was like reading our life story, trying to figure out the ending before I was only halfway through the book!

The driver introduced himself as 'Cody', slipping Adam a card with his details, and told us if we needed a guy to show us around L.A. then he was 'the man' and we only had to give him a call and he would be delighted to take us to see the Hollywood sights *et cetera*.

Very helpful, I thought, as I was hoping to visit the shopping mall and maybe an art gallery and book shop while Adam was visiting the corporation headquarters.

It was going to take twenty minutes to reach the hotel destination, so we sat back in Cody's yellow taxicab and soaked in the different sights along the route, the gently swaying palm trees that lined the streets, the neon-lit cafés and restaurants, the people rushing and the traffic buzzing. It was a different world!

On reaching the Marina hotel reception we were offered hot chocolate chip cookies in a brown paper bag by the receptionist who greeted us warmly as we entered the lobby. The cool air-conditioned reception was furnished in pale green and cream with palm, and ferns dotted around. It was very welcoming. The desk clerk gave us the card to room twenty-two on the ground floor, overlooking the pool, and pointed us in the direction of our suite.

My first thought was to phone Thomas and Ben and tell them we had arrived safely. The time difference between the UK and the US was eight hours, so Ben should be just getting up.

Thomas had offered to stay for the week with Ben, as Ben had never liked being on his own at Battlefields, not since the *Gallee* incident. He had insisted the unfinished portrait of the young boy was taken down before we left – and if he'd had his way, it would have been sitting at the local tip with all the other rubbish long ago.

I tapped in the number for Ben's mobile and he answered within two rings. 'Hi mum!'

It was good to hear his voice. Even though we had not been away more than twenty-four hours, it seemed as if it had been longer.

'How is everything?' he said.

I told him briefly about the amazing journey over and our encounter with Robbie Williams on the flight. He laughed and said I should have got a selfie! I explained that although I was desperate to get his autograph, I drew the line at invading his privacy beyond that.

Thomas came on the line and asked me about Los Angeles and what it was like. I told him as much as I could in a few brief sentences and almost played down the excitement I felt inside. I knew they would love it over here. It was an exciting place to come for a holiday, great to experience a whole new culture, and the amazing sunshine was a golden gift from the gods, but . . . To live here permanently . . . well!

I eventually rang off, promising to phone the next day with an update.

Adam went to take a shower and freshen up and I went to the window to look out. Beyond the pool area I could see the marina, where yachts and speed boats were bobbing up and down like champagne corks on a turquoise lily pond, their little flags fluttering in the gentle breeze. The sky was azure-blue and the sunshine an intense yellow. Down in the pool two little children were splashing each other while their mother watched in quiet amusement from her white wicker chair, a book on her lap and a cool cocktail in one hand.

I could have been on another planet. I knew the weather back home was poor, Ben had said it was raining, and more was predicted for the coming week. I felt guilty that the boys were having to endure it while we basked in the Californian sunshine. I wished they were here to enjoy the experience with us. That evening we ate in the hotel; we were tired from our long haul flight and Adam needed to be up at 7am to get to Corporate which meant a journey of twenty minutes or so depending on the flow of traffic. I planned to make use of the pool, reading, sunbathing and generally leading a very idyllic lifestyle.

The first morning I strolled across from the hotel to the local convenience store, and by the time I had got there I was glad to get out of the heat and into the cool, air-conditioned shop. I bought myself a sunhat and a bottle of water from the vending machine and a paperback.

After that I wandered around the local area for an hour, then returned to the hotel pool to start my new book. The day passed quickly, and it was not long before Adam returned from meeting Al and the team he would be working with if he accepted this new position and joined me outside on the veranda. I was eager to hear all his news, but he suggested going out for a meal and wanted to talk it all through over dinner.

He had done some research locally and had been recommended a place to eat at the end of the Santa Monica pier for dinner. I showered and changed from my swimwear into shorts and T-shirt, Adam into something more relaxing, we then walked across to the line of yellow taxis outside the hotel. After giving our destination to the cab driver, we were driven along the Pacific Highway for a few miles.

The palm trees swayed in the warm breeze along the coastline, which was incredible with the sapphire-blue sea and the golden beaches stretching for miles into the distance. Even though it was late in the afternoon, people were dotted along the white sandy shoreline sunbathing and relaxing. Teenagers played volleyball on the warm sand and children built sandcastles and paddled in the sea, while their parents stretched out enjoying the late afternoon sunshine.

My thoughts immediately went to Thomas and Ben back at Battlefields. What would they make of all this? It would be an incredible life for them, but would it be a good move for me?

Our short journey came to an end as the taxi pulled into a car park in Santa Monica next to the long wooden pier. We hopped out and after settling the taxi fare, walked across the car park and climbed the wooden stairway on to the boardwalk high above the beach. The pier stretched far into the sea, so we strolled along the weatherworn planks, taking in the sights and smells. Small stalls dotted the wooden pier selling postcards, American flags of all sizes, wooden puppets, candyfloss, giant lollypops, buckets and spades, along with hotdog stands and gigantic hotdogs with yellow mustard, candyfloss, cold slushies and ice cream! At the far end of the jetty, a steel band was playing Calipso music while happy granddads with their young grandchildren fished off the side of the pier. Thomas would love that!

The diner we were heading for was called 'Bubba Gump's' and it turned out to be a trendy seafood restaurant. There was a large five-foot pink plastic shrimp outside the main entrance with a smiling pink prawn face, sporting a red sailor's cap set at a jaunty angle, pointing the way in. The board outside boasted of a family chain of restaurants and boasted of selling 'THE BEST OF FRESH SEAFOOD AND AMERICAN FARE'. It sounded too good to be true!

The seating was in a fishing themed setting and had red leather couches lined up like couches in an old-fashioned train compartment. The restaurant had been running since 1996; it was busy with customers and had an American buzz about the place. Photographs were dotted around the wall with pictures of the making of the film *Forrest Gump* with Tom Hanks. I had watched it back in the UK and could see the similarities to the restaurant that Tom Hanks or Forrest Gump had used in the film. It was all very exciting and I took a few pictures to send back to Thomas and Ben.

As soon as the waitress saw us, she headed over and with a big ruby-red smile, introduced herself as Masey. We were shown to a little table for two with a red-and-white check tablecloth. The menu was printed on pink card depicting deep-fried mouthwatering coconut shrimp, side salads and crisps, which Masey explained were chips in England. She had obviously come across folk from the UK before and had anticipated our confusion over the *chips* or *crisps* as she called them.

She asked us what we would like to drink and recommended the iced lemon tea. It came in a larger-than-life glass full of ice, emblazoned with the *Bubba Gump* logo on the side, and Masey asked if we would like to buy the glasses to keep as a memento to take back home. Adam thought this was a great idea to give the boys as a gift so we said we would. She would make sure the glasses were wrapped for us at the end of our meal so we could take them home safely.

After ordering the basket of coconut prawns and side salad we sat looking out at the sea and the setting sun. This was such a treat and once again I pictured Thomas and Ben sitting there with us enjoying the experience.

The coconut prawns lived up to our expectations and melted in our mouths leaving a fried coconut taste in our mouths, we washed them down with the cold refreshing iced tea.

We stayed for more than an hour just soaking up the experience and then reluctantly called Masey to let her know we had finished. She told us not to forget our *Bubba Gump* glasses, which 'would be waiting at the exit door. Just hand the receipt to the young boy at the desk and he will have the glasses bagged up for you,' she said as she smiled.

Adam glanced at the receipt and was staggered to find the charge for the glasses had been added on to the bill and we were being charged ten dollars per glass! I told him not to worry – it was our own fault as we should have asked the price.

Adam felt a bit annoyed as we left the restaurant swinging the *Bubba Gump* carrier bag with the two new large *Bubba Gump* glasses safely wrapped in tissue paper.

We wandered to the end of the pier where there was a Ferris wheel and a roller coaster whizzing round a track. Screaming children were waving their arms in the air as they were flung side to side as the cars rose and dipped in a figure of eight.

A disc jockey was sitting on a high stool with music decks on a section of the pier. It was something to behold and quite amusing as all the people dancing were wearing earphones and we could not hear the music as it was being piped to the headphones of each of the dancers. They moved in unison as the beat took them on a musical journey that only they could hear. Some were on rollerblades, the girls in bikinis or T-shirts and shorts, the boys in sneakers and swimming trunks or cut-off jeans in the warm evening light, but all were having such fun.

We sat and watched for twenty minutes and then wandered back along the pier to find a taxi back to the hotel. What a day I had had!

The next morning Adam was off to corporate again, after a pancake stack drooling with thick brown maple syrup, a plate of fresh fruit consisting of the biggest blueberries I had ever seen, strawberries redder than the brightest red and oranges sweeter than I could have imagined, followed by pastries that would have been happy sitting on the pastry stand in a royal palace. Finally, after two cups of coffee Adam was gone, waving and smiling as he disappeared out of the hotel and into a yellow taxicab.

My day had been planned with only me in mind, so I had the morning to myself. I wandered over to the bookshop just across the road and was welcomed by a bright young female with a swinging ponytail standing by the door. She wore red-and-white checked, three-quarter length shorts and a white frilly blouse and the pinkest lipstick I had ever seen.

'Hi!' she said as she smiled sweetly at me, revealing a row of perfect white teeth, beautifully aligned with a silver train-track brace. 'Let me know if there is anything I can do to help. I'm Mandy.'

I thanked her and said I would.

'Are you from England?' she asked with eyes that opened so wide I could almost see my own reflection in them!

I told her I was and that I was just browsing and looking for something to take back for my sons as gifts. She recommended going to the upstairs floor where children's books were stored, but after explaining that my sons were young adults she giggled and apologised and sent me off in a different direction to peruse.

'I recommend aisle four,' she called after me as I turned the corner into aisle three! *These Americans can't do enough to help!* I thought.

After spending an hour or so looking at the huge choice of books I purchased two that I thought Ben and Thomas might enjoy and an autobiography for Adam. I made my way back to the over-helpful assistant and made my purchases.

'Is there anything else I can do for you?' she asked as she packed the paperbacks into a carrier bag. I thanked her kindly but declined her overzealous offer and, on leaving the shop, heard her call out, 'Have a nice day!'

That done I next entered a beautiful little store opposite called *The Pier*. As I opened the glass door, an aroma hit me full in the face with an overpowering infusion of warm cedarwood, sea salt and pine wood. It was the nicest fragrance I had ever smelt in my life.

A female voice called to me from somewhere deep in the shop. 'Feel free to browse and if there is anything you need or any questions answered, I'm up here and happy to help.'

'Thank you,' I called back, not actually seeing who I was conversing with. I could tell from her accent she was Scottish and, after sniffing all the diffusers to try and locate the intense aroma I had first smelt when entering the shop, I walked up to the till. I had already decided that I must have a bottle to take back home, or maybe two.

The shop assistant popped up from behind the counter like a rabbit out of a magician's top hat and beamed at me. Her hair was tied in a multicoloured silk scarf, and long greying ringlets hung down either side of her face. Her false eyelashes were longer than necessary, and her red blusher had been applied with a larger-than-average blusher brush. She must have been in her seventies but was dressed like a hippy from the sixties!

I asked her if the aroma wafting around the shop was on sale as it was such a lovely smell and she nodded vigorously, her ringlets bobbing up and down.

'Come this way' she said as she led me down the shop to a shelf full of perfumes and sprays beautifully displayed in flower-printed boxes. She picked up a tester bottle and squirted a fine scented mist in a circular motion all the way around my head. My eyes followed the tiny mist droplets until she stopped wafting the scent and I breathed in the ring of fragrance. It was intoxicating!

'Breathe,' she said as she wafted the scent in my direction. I took in the heady aroma. 'That's the one,' I said. 'It's gorgeous!'

After explaining the make-up of this scent and the various

ingredients used to produce it, she showed me several other products that she thought I might like. Hand soap, pillow spray and drawer liners – I bought the lot! *Adam would be impressed by her up-selling skills*, I thought.

The overpowering smell of this fragrance had drawn me in and seduced me. The shop owner, as she turned out to be, gave me her card and told me I could order any product online from anywhere in the world and it would be delivered to my door.

She put all my purchases into a pretty carrier bag along with a few pink crystals for my well-being. I thanked her, and just out of curiosity and with a lot of time on my hands, I commented on her Scottish accent. She was happy to tell me that she had come over to California from Glasgow on holiday when she was thirty, along with her husband, and had fallen head over heels in love with the Californian way of life, the sunshine and the people. They had decided to sell their aromatherapy business and home back in Scotland and invest in the Californian dream. It had all worked out well and they had not looked back.

I could tell she had made the right decision and was very happy.

After a few pleasantries I thanked her for *The Pier* experience, wished her success and bid her farewell She hoped I would enjoy my time in Los Angeles and wished me a happy life. As I left the shop, she called out, 'Have a nice day!'

The rest of the day was spent enjoying the Californian sunshine by the pool, waiting for Adam to return.

CHAPTER 23

THE CHEESECAKE FACTORY

That night we went to *The Cheesecake Factory* as a special treat. It was highly recommended by Al, and we were both very excited as we left the hotel in a taxi to try out this restaurant.

We entered through automatically opening glass doors emblazoned with *The Cheesecake Factory* logo at eye level. Just in case you did not know where you were! It was buzzing inside!

I could not believe my eyes as I took in the large glass display cabinets at the front of the restaurant, displaying an array of mouthwatering desserts, each one was labelled, there was Cookie Dough Lover's cheesecake with pecans, Coconut Cream Pie, Godiva Chocolate Cheesecake, Triple Berry Bliss and Lemon Meringue Cheesecake to name but a few. I counted thirty-six different varieties. It blew my mind, and I wondered which ones Ben and Thomas would have chosen if they had been here.

Young waitresses and waiters were zipping around the place carrying trays of delightful-looking food plates, stacked high with steak, lobster or fish dishes. One went past carrying a plate with the biggest piece of blueberry cheesecake that I had ever seen. It must have measured eight inches high. The tables were overflowing with delicious-looking mouthwatering food of every description.

We were shown to a table outside on the wooden decking overlooking the marina, where the reflection of the lights from the restaurant danced over the waves breaking around the harbour. It was magical! There were large fire-pits dotted across tiered decks, casting their flames into the star-studded black night sky, and we sat there looking at each other, smiles on our faces, wondering what the other was thinking.

Well, tonight was to be enjoyed whatever we decided about our future. We tucked into the most delicious meal of lobster, salad and French fries, followed by a piece of the famous strawberry cheesecake and two margaritas each. Feeling rather tipsy Adam paid the bill and we headed out past the happy chatting customers tucking into huge portions of cheesecake.

The evening went quickly and, after a long slow walk around the marina watching the luxurious yachts and the twinkling stars in the moonlit sky, we headed a little unsteadily to the taxi stand and back to the hotel for the evening.

The following day Adam organised a trip to a local art gallery for me. I boarded a yellow cab from outside the hotel after waving him off to go to corporate headquarters. Today was going to be a big day for Adam – he was not only spending time with Al but was meeting Al's boss for the first time. I knew he wanted to make a good impression and had spent the previous evening telling me all about the new position they were offering him.

I was looking forward to hearing about his day later that

night, but today I was on my own exploring an art gallery in Santa Monica.

I gave my destination to the cabbie, who opened the rear car door for me, and I jumped in. The journey took twenty minutes and was peppered with a few brief conversations along the way.

We drew up at what looked like a disused railway station, and I paid the fare and got out. I was not sure this was the right place as there wasn't a sign or entry point to the premises that I could see.

I was a bit concerned as the taxi drove off, leaving me feeling a little lost and vulnerable. Here I was in the middle of a strange city in an empty station, not knowing anybody and unsure of where to go. I suddenly felt out of my depth and wanted the reassurance of Adam's presence, but really did not want to phone him and concern him about my situation.

I pulled myself together and purposefully strode in the direction of a likely entrance on the side of the building. I opened the faded red door and stepped inside, it squeaked as I let it swing shut behind me. It was quiet and dimly lit but I plucked up courage and called out, 'Hello, is anybody there?'

I heard a scuffling noise and somebody called back, 'Come on through!' The voice sounded friendly and belonged to a woman who was sitting behind a small table tapping into a laptop in the middle of an adjoining room. The large window behind her let in a stream of sunlight and opened out on to a large yard containing sculptures of various design.

At least I am in the right place, I thought to myself.

She welcomed me into the room and went on to explain how the gallery was run. It was divided into three sections:

the sculpture courtyard, the art gallery and the photography section. She gave me a leaflet and pointed to the way into the photography section. It was free and if I had any questions, she would be happy to help.

I wandered through and found myself in a large, white-walled room studded with framed pictures of a bygone era. Hollywood was laid out in front of me in the form of black-and-white images depicting famous celebrities going back to the 1940s. They included all the Hollywood greats: Humphrey Bogart, Katharine Hepburn, John Wayne, Marilyn Monroe, Elizabeth Taylor, Robert Wagner, Frank Sinatra and so on and so on.

I could see in the background of many photographs the iconic palm trees of California, the beaches and the film sets and restaurants where these celebrities hung out. It was quite surreal to think that we might be living here in the future where it all happened, if we made the decision to emigrate.

I fancied a coffee after spending an hour in the photographic section, so I found a little café where there were pink Formica tables and yellow chairs and sat down to drink my cappuccino.

I wanted to share my excitement with someone and decided to call Ben and Thomas and share experience with them. Their voices made me feel a longing for home as I was missing them so much and talking to them both I wished I could see them in person, see their expressions when I told them about our time in California and the art gallery.

They were happy that we were having a great time exploring and told me they were missing us just as much and were looking forward to seeing us when we arrived back in the UK.

After disconnecting the call, I wandered outside to the

courtyard where there was amazing, if unusual, sculptures relating to the fact that the art area was situated in a disused railway station. Twisted iron rails that once paved the way for the railroad to cross the West were bent into large sculptural words. Rusting tin palm trees lined the courtyard walls and huge lollipops of bright colours were dotted around, creating an eclectic mix of artwork.

The rest of my time was spent perusing the huge array of abstract, contemporary and pop art, which I found fascinating. After three hours of indulgence, I made my way to the exit and wandered out into the hot sunshine.

The heat of the outside helped me make a quick decision as to what I was going to do next – and that was to return to the hotel pool! I walked out of the yard and hailed a taxicab, just like they do in the Hollywood movies, and sped off back to the hotel.

The afternoon was spent dipping in and out of the cool water, applying lots of factor-thirty suncream and reading the new novel I had picked up at the bookstore.

Adam was full of exciting news about his time at corporate when he got back to the hotel and took me to another fancy Mexican restaurant a short drive along the freeway. He told me of his experience with Al and his boss when they took him to an American sports bar for lunch, where they had enjoyed chicken and chips and watched American football on the big screen for an hour. He wondered if it was like that all the time or whether this was just to show him what American life would be like if he accepted their job offer.

We had a lot to discuss and neither of us was stating a

preference as to whether we should come to the US permanently or not. We were exploring all the options and would wait until we got home to come to a decision either way.

The good thing was we had time to ourselves for the next two days and Adam had a few ideas as to where we should visit.

The following morning, we woke up to bright blue skies and warm sunshine yet again. I was enthusiastic to start out after an enormous breakfast of stringy bacon, hash browns, over-easy fried egg, followed by warm croissants with butter and raspberry jam and a plate of fresh fruit, consisting of strawberries, mango, blueberries and pineapple slices. It was finally washed down with a freshly squeezed orange juice and a latte to follow.

Our plan was to hire a car and go to the Getty Museum. It was somewhere I had put on my list of places of interest when doing research on the area and even though it was an hour's drive away, it was along the interstate and not difficult to get there. Adam was happy to drive and so we set off for the day.

With the air-conditioning on and music on the radio we were in high spirits and entered the interstate, where Adam expertly negotiated the five lanes of traffic to our destination.

On arrival we left the car parked under a tree and caught a monorail to the top of the cliff where the Getty building was situated. It was an amazing building with fantastic views of the city of Los Angeles. The gardens were over many levels with white pathways of tiny stone Cacti and a variety of huge succulents and orchids of all colours festooned the whole area, creating a rooftop of flowers. It was such a sight.

The interior was modern and had glass walls everywhere

so you could enjoy the spectacular views from inside as well as outside. We wandered round enjoying all that there was on offer and finally had lunch sitting on a little table for two looking over the city.

Adam wanted to catch up with Thomas and Ben, so he used his mobile and got through to them. They were having breakfast and were excited to hear from us.

Ben asked what we were doing today so Adam told him all about the last few days' excursions and explained that we were on top of a cliff overlooking Los Angeles. I could hear Ben asking if we were going to live in California, but Adam was giving no indication one way or the other. The rest of the phone call was spent catching up with what they had been doing, and we finally ended the conversation with a promise to phone again the following day.

The afternoon we travelled along the Pacific Highway, stopping off at several beaches and walking barefoot along the edge of the waves that pounded the golden shores of the State.

The following day was to be our last, so we decided to end it in style. We got up early and headed out to Malibu along the Pacific Coast Highway, with a picnic of cheeses, pickles, fresh baguettes and fresh fruit, oh, and a bottle of Californian white wine to celebrate our final few hours.

The area we headed to was just off the highway and was called Paradise Beach. It took us half an hour to find but it was worth the effort. Backed by sand dunes, the golden beach stretched far into the distance, the glistening surf crashed on to the shore where surfers negotiated the breaking waves as they tumbled in, and the hot sunshine shone down on us for the last time.

We had had an incredible time here in California but we both knew we were going to have to make some tough decisions about whether we leave the UK and make our home here in Los Angeles or whether to stay in Battlefields and continue our lives in England. I looked at Adam lying on the beach soaking up the sunshine. What was he thinking?

CHAPTER 24

RETURN TO BATTLEFIELDS

The following day we were up early, check-out was by ten from the hotel, but we were ready by nine for our final journey in a yellow taxicab to the airport. We pulled our heavy cases down the hallway, full of gifts for Thomas and Ben and a few friends. I had even thought of Jessica back home while shopping previously and had purchased a beautiful book for her on succulents. I thought I could give it to her as a parting gift if we left Battlefields and that she might enjoy cultivating cacti in the new greenhouse and think of me occasionally.

The Battlefields hallway would be overgrown with large cacti and potted palms, probably much to the annoyance and distain of Francesco.

I wondered how things had been while we were away and if there were calm seas or storm clouds brewing on our return. Life had been difficult at times, sometimes hilarious and sometimes quite exasperating living with so many different personalities at Battlefields, but it was where we had made our home for the past few years.

I knew deep down that Adam had moved to Battlefields for

me, really, and had on more than one occasion mentioned that life could be simpler if we lived somewhere else. This new job offer had come out of the blue and had given us a lot to think about for the future.

After catching up with Thomas on his mobile and learning that Ben had found himself a new girlfriend while we had been away, we boarded the return flight to Heathrow on Air New Zealand once again. The journey back was just as comfortable and the attention from the stewardess just as attentive and professional as it had been on the flight over. Alas, there was no Michael to attend to my every need but hey ho!

We touched down eleven hours and fifteen minutes later and got through customs without too much fuss. The electronic passport control held Adam up for a few minutes but at least the luggage was delivered back safely to us in the arrivals lounge twenty minutes later via a trolley and a very smart man called Stewart.

We made our way through the airport to the exit where we were disappointed to find it had started raining outside. The Californian sunshine would become a long distant memory if we stayed at Battlefields.

I was still undecided as to a decision when we left the airport and travelled home, as to where my heart lay. The car journey was uneventful, the motorway stretched into the distance and spray and water from the lorries and cars engulfed us as we headed to number three.

Finally, after a few long hours, we turned into the lane leading down the drive to Battlefields House. Adam went to turn off the radio just as the DJ introduced the Beach Boys and 'California

Girls' as the next song. Adam looked at me and started laughing, then I started laughing!

We sat in the car park as the rain hammered down, listening to the Beach Boys, both lost in our thoughts.

'Penny for them,' said Adam.

'Mmmmm . . .' I said.

ACKNOWLEDGEMENTS

The author would like to thank Douglas, Frances and the team at SPP Brown Dog Books for their help in producing Battlefields House. Without their help and support the journey from pen to print would have been impossible.

ABOUT THE AUTHOR

The author Diane Davies was born in Clifton, Bristol and grew up in Avonmouth. She went onto higher education later in life after bringing up two sons and attended Bath Spa University where she spent three years studying for a BA(HONS) Degree in 3D Design in Ceramics. Her love of writing goes back to childhood and her passion for books. Her first novel Battlefields House was written after a period of time spent living at Battlefields House, near Bath with her husband and youngest son. The author now lives in Wickwar, Wotton-Under-Edge, Gloucestershire with her husband Ian. She continues to write short stories for children based on her travels, where she gains inspiration for characters and storylines.